Ace

The Rebellion Series

Nicola Jane

Copyright © 2019 (original) Ace by Nicola Jane

Copyright © 2023 (Updated) Ace by Nicola Jane

All rights reserved.

No portion of this book may be reproduced in any form without written permission from the publisher or author, except as permitted by U.K. copyright law.

Meet The Team

♥

Cover design: Francessca Wingfield -Wingfield Designs

Editor: Rebecca Vazquez, Dark Syde Books

Formatting: Nicola Miller

Spelling Note

Please note, this author resides in the United Kingdom and is using British English. Therefore, some words may be viewed as incorrect or spelled incorrectly, however, they are not.

Trigger Warning

I don't feel this book needs a trigger warning. If you read Mafia/MC romance, you already know what to expect.

NICOLA JANE

But for the people out there who require one, consider yourself warned. This book isn't for the faint-hearted.

Acknowledgments

♥

Although this is one of my first MC books, it still gets a lot of love. So, thank you to my readers who continue to follow my journey and read whatever I write, old and new.

Trigger Warning

As with all my books, this story comes with a trigger warning. It contains violence, sex, alpha males, terrible language and kidnap and assault scenes (Although the author does not go into detail)

Contents

Playlist	IX
Chapter One	1
Chapter Two	15
Chapter Three	29
Chapter Four	42
Chapter Five	57
Chapter Six	72
Chapter Seven	83
Chapter Eight	95
Chapter Nine	108
Chapter Ten	123
Chapter Eleven	134

Chapter Twelve	146
Chapter Thirteen	162
Chapter Fourteen	175
Chapter Fifteen	188
Chapter Sixteen	200
Chapter Seventeen	214
Chapter Eighteen	231
Chapter Nineteen	245
Chapter Twenty	259
Chapter Twenty-One	274
Chapter Twenty-Two	285
A note from me to you	290
Books by Nicola Jane	291

Playlist

♥

A Drop In The Ocean – Ron Pope
Give Me Love – Ed Sheeran
Love You From a Distance – Ashley Kutcher
Thinking 'Bout Love – Wild Rivers

Age Ain't Nothing But a Number – Aaliyah
Just a Friend to You – Meghan Trainor
The Heart Wants What It Wants – Selena Gomez
Almost Is Never Enough – Ariana Grande ft. Nathan Sykes
Half Of You – Grace Carter
Forever Young – Audra Mae

NICOLA JANE

(I Can't Help) Falling In Love With You – UB40

Chapter One

ACE

The guy shifts under my heavy boot as I press down on his windpipe. "It's simple really." I sigh, lighting my cigarette and inhaling. "You keep your hands to yourself and show respect. Which part did you not get?"

He coughs violently, reaching for my boot and tapping like he's in a wrestling match. "Please," he croaks, desperately trying to refill his lungs.

"Come on, Pres, we're wasting time." Scar pats my shoulder.

"I'm a little busy," I growl.

NICOLA JANE

"The wedding starts in ten minutes. Lucy will have your balls if we're late."

At the mention of my daughter's name, I feel instant happiness and lift my boot from the guy's neck. He scrabbles to his feet, gasping. I grip his shirt collar and haul him to me so I can look him in the eyes. "Stay away from Angel," I warn. "You two are finished. Pack your shit up today and be gone by the time I drop her home tonight." He nods, and I shove him away from me like the dirty shitbag he is.

"Get me to my girl," I say, smiling at Scar.

"What's the deal with you and Angel anyway, Pres? Are you claiming her?" he asks as we head over to our bikes.

I laugh. I've never claimed an old lady, and I have no intention of doing it now. "Nah, she needed my help. She turned up at the club last night all beat up and shit."

"She's a club whore, Pres, what does it matter?"

I stop walking and glare at Scar. "Watch your mouth, brother. Club whore, old lady, cook, cleaner . . . who gives a fuck? Men don't beat up on women, and in my club, everyone is important."

ACE

Scar gives a quick nod before throwing a leg over his bike. I don't ask much from my guys at the Rebellion MC, just that they show respect for one another and look out for everyone, and that includes the club whores.

We drive straight to the church where my daughter, Lucy, is marrying Matteo Corallo, also known as Tag. He's a good man, an MMA fighter and crime boss with Mafia connections that run deep. He can look after my girl, and seeing as she's only been back in my life for a year, it gives me peace to know she's happy.

We park the bikes and head towards the groups of people gathering outside. I shake hands with a few of the associates from various Mafia families. Since the death of their Capo, Conner Martinez, we've been doing more and more business together. Conner's son, and Tag's friend, Anton, is now heading up the organisation, and let's just say, I trust him a hell of a lot more than I did his father.

I head inside and take a seat in the back pew with the rest of the Rebellion. When Lucy announced her marriage to

NICOLA JANE

Tag, I didn't expect an invite, mainly because her mother, Sylvia, hates me.

I met her when I was sixteen. I was a cocky, womanizing teenager, and she was a rich bitch. I had the world at my feet, or so I thought, jumping from one woman's bed to the next. But when she announced she was pregnant, she floored me. Nevertheless, I offered to do the right thing, but she turned her snooty nose up at me, telling me her parents would never approve. She was destined to marry a rich man, and from what Lucy tells me, she did just that. I spent a long time after that thinking I wasn't good enough, that I was scum because of my lifestyle.

Sylvia let me have contact with Lucy for the first year, just occasionally, whenever she could sneak away from her parents. But eventually, she met another guy and told me I couldn't see Lucy again. I walked away without a fight, the biggest regret I've ever had. Getting Lucy back is a blessing, and I'll never let her out of my life again.

My son, Hulk, slides along the pew. "I hate churches. Am I the only one who feels like I'm gonna get struck down at the doorway?"

ACE

I laugh. "Even God can't strike me down today. I'm the happiest man alive right now."

Hulk rolls his eyes. "Married to the Mafia, what's to be happy about?"

"You like Tag, so shut the fuck up."

He smirks. "I like the money the club makes from him."

People begin to stand, so we follow their lead. The music begins to play, and I straighten my kutte. Lucy insisted we wear them, saying we should never hide who we are.

I inhale sharply as she steps into the church. She looks stunning, like an angel floating down the aisle. Next to her stands her stepfather. I don't begrudge him the right to walk my girl down the aisle because, as Lucy explained, he raised her since she was ten years old, and I'm happy just to be here to see this whole thing happen.

Lucy catches my eye, and I give her a small wave. She halts her step and then unhooks her arms from her stepfather. I hear her whisper an apology before asking him to wait for one second. She holds out her hand to me. "Why are you sitting back here?" she asks, grabbing my hand firmly in hers.

NICOLA JANE

"I'm just fine back here," I explain, but she shakes her head.

"No, you and Hulk belong at the front." I look back at Hulk, who scowls at me. He pretends he hates Lucy, but I know he's warming to her.

I let her lead us down the aisle with everyone staring wide-eyed. She makes the guests in the second row shuffle along the pew until there's enough room for me and Hulk to squeeze in. She kisses us both on the cheek and then marches back towards her stepfather, uttering words of apology to the guests. My wide smile falters when I notice that Sylvia is glaring at me from the row in front. Hulk finds the whole thing hilarious and nudges me, grinning. I flip him off, making sure it's behind the pew so Sylvia can't see.

The ceremony is over quickly. We have Tag to thank for that because he didn't want to get married in a church. His original plan was to whisk Lucy away to the Caribbean, but she said her mother would never forgive her. The one thing we all agreed on was that the party was just as important as the ceremony. Lucy asked if we could host it at the clubhouse, much to Sylvia's disgust, and as we walk round the back of the clubhouse, I know I made the right decision to hire the large white marquee.

A waiter stands at the entrance, a tray of full Champagne glasses balanced carefully. I went all out on this, despite Lucy wanting to organise it herself. She is a wedding planner after all. But I didn't want Sylvia to think I couldn't afford to pay for my daughter's wedding, and I knew Lucy would go cheap, worrying about the cost. In the end, Sylvia paid for the church, and I took care of the party.

The marquee fills up with guests and I overhear the occasional comment about the flower centrepieces on each table and the twinkling fairy lights placed around the tent. I don't know what they expected from a biker wedding, but class was the only way I was gonna go with Sylvia and her husband looking down their noses at me.

A Rolls Royce slows to a stop outside the tent, and I stay by the entrance to welcome the newly married couple. Sylvia appears at my side, and I stiffen. "Max."

"Sylvia."

"The marquee is lovely."

NICOLA JANE

"Thank you. I wanted the best for Lucy."

"Well, the best isn't a marquee, but I understand that Lucy wanted to include you. It was important to her."

"I told her she could have a castle if she wanted. She asked to have it here." I feel annoyed by her judgemental tone, but before we can get into a full-blown argument, Lucy throws her arms around me and kisses my cheek. "I love it, Dad. It's exactly what I pictured," she gushes, and I give Sylvia an 'I told you so' look.

MAE

Relaxing back into my chair, I've eaten far too much, and I feel sick and sluggish. A good nap is needed to recover from this. My dress is not the kind of forgiving material required for a wedding, but it is perfect for the endless pictures we've had taken, as it holds everything in and enhances my curves. Piper hands me a glass of Champagne, which I place straight on the table. I hate the stuff and only ever drink it to be polite or when a toast is raised.

"Ace did good," says Piper, and I agree. For a badass scary biker, the guy sure did pull off this party.

ACE

I stare at him across the dance floor. His broad shoulders, bulging biceps, tattoos, speckles of grey in his hair, and the bright blue of his eyes all give me thoughts that I definitely shouldn't be thinking about the club's President. "Earth to Mae," says Piper, waving her hand in front of my dazed face. "Are you dreaming about Scar?" she asks, screwing up her face.

"No." I sigh, realising that Ace is chatting with Scar, so he would be the obvious guess.

"Good, because I hear bad things about that man."

"Just like I hear bad things about Hulk, yet you still dream about him." I smirk, my tone teasing.

Piper scowls at me. She's fancied Lucy's brother since she was a teenager, way before Lucy came into our lives. Hulk uses her over and over, but she can never seem to tell him no. "I use him purely for sex," she snaps.

"He uses *you* purely for sex. You love him."

"Don't be ridiculous. Number one rule, never . . ." she begins, and we both laugh and complete the sentence together, "fall in love with a biker."

NICOLA JANE

A shadow falls over our table and I look up into the eyes of Ace. My insides do a flip, and I subconsciously suck in my stomach. It's not that I'm fat, but I'm not the super slim size of Piper or Lucy. Ace holds out a whiskey on the rocks to me, and I take it gratefully. "Thanks, Pres." I smile at how he knows me too well.

"You girls enjoying the night?"

"It's been amazing from start to finish," gushes Piper. "Oh, there's Nova, I'll be back." And then she rushes off, leaving me alone with Ace.

He lowers his huge body into the vacated seat and his eyes pierce me. "You look amazing today, Mae," he says, and those damn butterflies in my stomach take flight again.

"You don't look too bad yahself, Ace." I smile, adding a wink. "How was it seeing Lucy's mum?" I know he was nervous about seeing her again. "I thought she was going to combust when Lucy moved you up front in the church."

He laughs, and his whole face smiles when he does that. "It was okay, just as I expected. She made some comment about Lucy choosing the club over something fancy, but

ACE

yah know what, Lucy's had a great day and that's all I wanted."

"Lucy isn't like her mum. She didn't want a big fancy wedding. If her own mother doesn't know that, it doesn't say much about their relationship," I point out.

"Why doesn't Sylvia see it like we do? Lucy was blown away with the marquee, but Sylvia made some comment about Lucy only agreeing to it to include me. Her comments are so condescending." He sighs.

"Seeing her again was the hardest part, but you got through it. Did you catch up with Angel's boyfriend?" I ask, keeping my tone light. The problem with me and Ace is we talk. He comes to me if he's worried or stressed because he says he finds me easy to talk to, and honestly, I like our secret chats. But then, when he gets jealous or he meets a new woman, he tells me all about that too, and that's not so much fun.

"He met the boot." He smirks. "Piece of shit."

"Speak of the devil," I mutter as Angel spots us and saunters over. If her skirt was any shorter, I'd get a view of her vagina for sure. I hate to admit it, but even with bruises, she's beautiful. Angel's boyfriend likes to get handy with his fists when he's had a drink, last night was one time too many for Ace, who's been sleeping with Angel for a few months. He finally stepped in, but I don't know what this kind of declaration means. Maybe he'll claim Angel and break my heart.

"Hey, Pres," she practically purrs.

"Angel." Ace grins, taking her fingers in his. "Let me know when you're ready to go, and I'll drop you home."

She lowers, almost shoving her cleavage in his face. Running her manicured red nails along his inner thigh, she whispers something into his ear. Ace closes his eyes and grins wide. "I'll look forward to it," he says and smirks. As she walks away, swaying her arse for extra measure, his eyes are glued to her, and I'm once again reminded of how he prefers his women super skinny with fake boobs, rubber lips, and arse implants.

"You may as well lay claim to her, Ace," I mutter, and he arches a brow. "Well, you beat up her ex, you drive her home, you pay for her plastic surgery . . . she's practically your wife."

"I prefer the single life, Mae, you know that," he says, throwing back his drink. "And I don't pay for her surgery. Who said I do?"

"She did. Said your words were 'you fuck her, and you want her to look her best'."

Ace laughs. "She said that? I'll slap her backside later." He grins, and I hold back the vomit in my mouth. The thought of him smacking her oversized fake arse pisses me off.

Ace pulls a small, silver hip flask from his inside pocket and unscrews the cap. He's about to put it to his mouth when I snatch it from his grasp and drink it myself. He watches with amusement when I wince at the strong flavour as it burns my insides. "What the hell is that?" I gasp.

"You'll regret that in about half an hour. It's strong," he laughs, "you're supposed to sip a small amount, savour the woody taste."

I hand it back and decide to get my own drink from the bar. I need to forget the images of Ace and Angel together.

NICOLA JANE

I'm halfway through a bottle of wine and aware that I look like a bitter drunk watching everyone have fun. The hardest thing about being in love with a powerful older man, who also happens to be your best friend's dad, is that you can't tell anyone why you're so miserable. I pour myself another glass and watch Ace and Angel holding hands as they leave. Sure looks like he's claiming her to me . . . and to everyone else in the room.

Chapter Two

♥

ACE

Angel steps off my bike outside her house and then runs her hand up my chest, unfastening the top button on my shirt. "Are you coming inside?" she purrs, running her tongue along her plumped lower lip.

"I guess I should check that your ex isn't inside waiting for you." I grin, tapping her backside.

I step through the door of her house, and she turns, throwing herself at me. I catch her, and she wraps her legs around my waist and tugs at my hair. "I need you now," she whispers, kissing me hard. I kick the door closed. I hate to be dominated, preferring my women gentle and submissive, not aggressive and pushy. But Angel has something about her that I just can't seem to stay away from, and she refuses to be tamed.

I hold her against the wall and place my hand around her throat. Her barely-there dress has risen up over her thighs and her panties are exposed. I rub my erection against her. "You need me, you'd better get on those knees and show me how bad," I growl, sliding her body down mine, lowering her feet to the ground.

Angel tugs at my belt, but my mobile rings from my pocket and she freezes. I always take the calls, no matter what I'm doing or where I am, because people only call me when they need my help.

"Yep?" I answer.

"Pres, sorry to bother you, but are you heading back here soon?" It's Queenie, one of the old ladies.

I sigh. "Is it urgent?"

"I can feel trouble brewing, and you said to call if anyone was starting anything."

"For fuck's sake, who is it?" I growl. I'd made sure all The Rebellion knew to be on their best behaviour today, and I made it clear there was to be no trouble at Lucy's wedding.

ACE

"Scar and one of the men from Tag's side."

There can't be any trouble between the MC and Mafia, not when we've come this far to begin working together. "Right, I'm on my way. Can't you get Mae to work her female charms to calm shit until I get there?"

"Sure," she sighs, "although she's looking a bit worse for wear."

"Is she okay?" I ask, concern in my voice. Mae is a good friend. She's level-headed, and she's my go-to person when I need to hear it straight.

"Yeah, don't worry, just get here."

I disconnect the call and give Angel an apologetic smile. "Sorry, darling, you know how it is." She sighs and rolls her eyes, another reminder of why I stay single. It takes an understanding woman to be my old lady.

I get back to the clubhouse, and Hulk makes his way over to me. "Don't worry, Piper sorted it," he mutters, and I follow his pissed-off glare in Piper's direction. She's dancing close to one of Tag's men, working her backside into his groin.

"To be fair to her, Hulk, I asked Queenie to get someone to work their charm to calm the situation until I could get here."

"And that involved dry humping him for all to see, did it?" snaps Hulk, not taking his eyes off the scene before him. "The girl always goes in full force. Can't she flirt without rubbing herself on him like an attention-seeking cat?"

I decide to ignore his moaning. He doesn't want Piper, but he doesn't want anyone else to have her either. "Is Mae okay? Queenie said she was a little worse for wear."

"She took a guy out back about five minutes ago." I glance around, hoping to hell she isn't with Scar. "Also Mafia," adds Hulk, and I don't know if that's worse or better.

"She's drunk. She shouldn't be making bad decisions. You should've stopped her," I mutter, irritated.

"She's young, free, and single. She should most definitely be making bad choices. Mae's boring and nothing like she should be for her age."

"She is not. Stop being a dick. I'm gonna go find her and check she's okay. You stay and watch these guys, and call me if anyone steps outta line."

I step out of the marquee and listen to see if I can hear voices. It's too loud with the music pumping and people's laughter filling the late-night air.

"Mae," I shout and then listen for a response. When she doesn't answer, I walk around the back of the marquee. "Mae," I shout again.

I hear a scuffle and whispers, then I spot two figures in the pitch black, their shadows close together. "Mae, is that you?" I repeat.

"Erm, yeah. I'm fine," she answers.

"Fuck being fine, who the hell are you out here with?" I move closer until I can see her face. The man with her is one of Tag's ringside team. I've seen him many times, usually with different women. "Get the hell back inside," I snap.

"Ace, I'm good," she hisses.

"You never said your dad was Ace." The guy smirks, and I picture my fist hitting his perfectly chiselled jaw line.

Mae giggles. "He's not. He's Lucy's dad."

"Mae, you're drunk, let's get you inside before you do something you'll regret."

"I won't regret it. I'm so sick of being the good girl everyone runs to with their problems," she slurs. "I want to be the girl who has one-night stands and drinks too much." She sways, and the guy grabs her to steady her.

He gives me an awkward smile. "I should go."

I roll my eyes and take her from him so he can make his escape. She tries to protest but slaps her hand over her mouth. "I feel sick," she mutters.

"Some party animal you're turning out to be," I tease, leading her back inside.

Mae's bedroom is on one of the upper floors and getting her up the stairs is a slow process. In the end, I tire of her clumsy steps and decide to throw her over my shoulder.

ACE

"Why did you get so drunk?" I growl, shaking my head in annoyance as I climb the rest of the stairs.

"To mend my broken heart," she whimpers.

"First, whoever broke your heart, I'll kill them, and second, did it work?"

"It's a secret, and no, it still hurts. Did I mention that I feel sick?"

I open her door and deposit her on her bed. "Get some sleep," I growl. She curls herself into a ball and groans. I hesitate and ask, "Are you gonna be okay?" She responds with another groan. "Mae, are you gonna be okay?"

She tries to sit herself up, almost falling off the edge of the bed. "I'm not ugly, am I?"

I shift uncomfortably. I've been in Mae's room many times, usually to vent when I'm ready to explode. She listens and doesn't judge, but she never talks about herself, her feelings, or shit like that, and I'm afraid she's gonna cry any minute. It's unfamiliar territory and something Piper would be better dealing with. I pull out my phone, hoping she can come up here. "Oh god, you think I am, don't you? It's because I'm so ugly!"

NICOLA JANE

I sigh. "No, you're not ugly." And I'm not just saying that to appease her—she really is beautiful. Her curves are perfect, she has the right amount of arse to breast, and she isn't one of those skinny girls with nothing on her bones. I like a girl who doesn't order a salad at a restaurant. Her dark hair falls to her backside in waves. "Where's this all coming from, Mae?" I tuck my phone away again.

"I know I'm not like Piper and Nova," she mutters. I sigh and take a seat beside her. "And I'm always the one everyone comes to for advice," she continues. "But sometimes, I just want a man to look at me and think, 'wow, she's stunning'."

"Mae, stop. This isn't like you. When you sober up, you'll feel better," I say, stroking her hand.

"I love someone," she whispers, "so bad, it hurts."

I've never seen Mae with a man. She just doesn't bother with all that stuff. "Does he feel the same?"

"He doesn't know how I feel. I'm scared to tell him in case I mess up our friendship."

"Any man would be honoured to have you love him, Mae. You should tell him."

ACE

"What if he doesn't feel the same?"

"Then it's his loss." I stand. "Sleep it off and everything will feel better tomorrow."

I head for the door. "Ace, I need to tell you something." My hand freezes on the door handle. "I know this seems weird and completely out of the blue—" I grip the handle tighter, hoping to god she's not about to say what I think she is.

"No," I hiss, turning to face her. "Don't say it. Don't finish that sentence," I warn. She's talking crazy. Mae is two years older than my own daughter. I knew her father. I watch in horror as she stands and wobbles her way towards me.

"You said to tell him," she cries.

"Mae, I'm fifteen years older than you."

"It's just a number."

"It is not just a number, otherwise, they wouldn't put age limits on shit."

MAE

NICOLA JANE

I see the confusion on Ace's face, but still, I keep talking, trying to convince him that my stupid crush is worth the risk. My brain is willing me to shut the fuck up, but as I get closer to him and inhale his spicy aftershave, I lunge forward, planting a kiss somewhere near his mouth but not close enough to get it on his lips. It's not how I'd pictured it going, and I wince at the horrified expression on his face.

"Say something," I whisper, but he continues to stare at me like I've grown an extra head, and then he backs out the room, closing the door firmly behind him so I don't follow. "Fuck," I mumble out loud. "Fuck, shit, fuck."

I crawl into bed, the awful messed-up feeling not leaving my stomach as I bury myself under my sheets. How will I ever face him after that mortifying confession?

By the morning, the shame hasn't left me. I clean my face of last night's makeup and drag a brush through my tangled hair. Then I pull on my workout clothes, needing to run off this hangover. I get downstairs to find a few of the

ACE

guys asleep on the couches. They won't rise until at least midday, but I'm sure Queenie and my mum, Bernie, will clear them off to their rooms once they're up and about. They like a tidy place.

I'm careful not to wake them as I sneak out. I was hoping Dodge, Ace's Staffordshire bull terrier dog, would be waiting for me. He's a rescue dog of sorts. Ace found him dumped on the industrial estate where the club is based. Dodge doesn't trust many people, but he loves me and will often come out for a run with me. I give a low whistle, but he still doesn't appear, and I wonder if Ace ended up going back to Angel's last night after I'd scared him off.

I run for half an hour. My lungs are burning, but the hangover is definitely clearing. As I round the last straight road home, Dodge comes bounding up to me, jumping around me excitedly. I stroke him, talking high-pitched and burying my face into his neck. I look up at Ace, who is also dressed in his running gear. "Hungover?" he asks.

"Not anymore," I mutter, standing straighter.

"Thought a run would clear my head," he says, his voice gravelly and low, "but it hasn't helped."

NICOLA JANE

"Look, about last night—" I begin, knowing it's better to face this shit head-on.

He shakes his head, cutting me off with his frostiness. "I don't want to ever discuss it again, Mae, not EVER! Is that clear?"

I'm taken aback. I know I caught him off guard, but seriously? "Let me just say—"

"NO!" he snaps, getting closer. "No. We're never gonna happen. I'm old enough to be your father. Lucy is only two years younger than you." He laughs bitterly and shakes his head. "What did you think would happen, Mae? That we'd run off happily into the sunset? You shouldn't have told me."

"You told me to," I protest.

"I didn't know you meant me."

"I can't help how I feel," I mumble.

"Don't. Don't do that sad face like I'm in the wrong here. I knew your father, Mae. We were friends when you were just a kid. Fuck, you still *are* a kid to me."

"I'm twenty-five, hardly a kid. You're overreacting, and you don't need to yell at me."

ACE

"You're my go-to, Mae. Who the fuck do I talk to now? You've ruined us."

"It doesn't have to be that way, Ace. You can still talk to me."

"How can I, knowing how you feel?" he asks, shaking his head.

"Nothing's changed."

He rolls his eyes. "Everything's changed. We can't be like we were ever again."

"Christ, you're acting like an idiot," I snap, and he arches his brow.

"What the fuck did you say to me?" I see his eyes change. The kind, soft man I'm used to switches to President, head of The Rebellion MC.

I square my shoulders; I've already started so I may as well carry on. "I'm not your fucking personal agony aunt. If I'm too young for you, maybe you shouldn't be running to me for advice whenever you can't handle shit."

"You need to watch your mouth. Don't forget who the fuck I am," he warns. He clicks his fingers and Dodge heels at his side. "And trust me, I won't be coming to you for anything, least of all advice." I watch as he storms off angrily.

Chapter Three

♥

ACE

"I wish that animal wouldn't sit on my couch," says Angel.

"You mean Dodge, my best friend?" I pant, thrusting my cock hard into her.

"Yes, he's laying all over my new throw."

I glance back at Dodge sprawled out and snoring on Angel's couch. "Why are you concerned about the damn dog when we're fucking?" I ask.

"He's distracting. You know I hate animals."

I place my hand over her mouth. I came here to fuck, not to discuss animal preferences. After my run and then my argument with Mae, I needed to work off my frustrations, but turns out, it isn't working too well for me.

Mae's hurt eyes flash through my mind, and I shake my head, trying to clear it. She's the last person I should be thinking about right now. I wrap Angel's hair around my fist and pull her head back so that I have access to her neck. Running my tongue along the skin, I gently nip until I reach her shoulder. "Anyone ever tell you that you talk too much?" I growl, because despite my hand covering her mouth, she's still trying to talk. I release her and then lower her feet to the ground. "Fight me," I order, and she rolls her eyes.

She sighs. "I'm not really in the mood to fight today, Ace." I tuck my semi-hard cock back into my pants, and she scowls. "What are you doing?"

"I need a good fuck. I'm not into boring married sex." I'm being a dick and taking out my bad mood on her, blaming her for my lack of erection.

"You can't go and fuck someone else," she snaps, and alarm bells ring.

ACE

I whistle to Dodge, and he immediately jumps up and heads my way. "You aren't my old lady, Angel, so don't act like you are." I need to quash that shit straight away. Now her ex is out the picture, there's no way I'm filling his shoes.

"Wait," she shouts, but I continue towards the door. She jumps in front of me and slaps me hard across the face. It takes me a second to work out whether she's playing or for real, but there's definite anger in her eyes. "I thought you wanted a fight!" She raises her hand again, but this time, I catch it and twist it behind her back, pushing her up against the door.

"That's much better," I hiss, releasing my cock again. I keep her pressed against the door, despite her feeble attempts to fight me off. "Now, keep that mouth shut!" Dodge seems to realise that I might be some time, so he heads back to the couch.

I push her to floor, all the while she struggles. I pin her arms above her head, and when she raises her knee to try and kick me away, I force her legs apart. "Safe word?" I pant.

"Fuck you," she spits.

NICOLA JANE

"Nope." I smirk, rubbing my cock against her entrance. She moans and instinctively raises her pussy to try and get me closer to her. "Harley," she eventually says. I thrust into her hard, and she yells out in surprise. Keeping her hands above her head, I pump into her, chasing my release.

When I get back to the club, I head straight for the shower. The sinking feeling in my stomach remains, and since Mae told me how she really feels, I can't seem to shake it. I dry off and pull on some jeans, then go back down to my office. I pass Queenie, who looks me up and down appreciatively. I know I have a good body, even at my age, and I'm not ashamed to have it on show. "I'm telling Bear that you're looking at me like that," I joke, and she laughs.

"That man needs to take a page out of your book and take his tired arse to the gym, then I might look at him the same way." She's joking—she loves Bear and his cuddly frame. "Hey, Ace, is Mae okay?" she suddenly asks.

"Erm, I dunno. Why would I know?" I feel like the entire club is suddenly aware of how she feels about me.

ACE

Queenie frowns, then shrugs. "No reason. She seems a little off, and I know she talks to you, so I thought she might have said something."

I shake my head, my mood suddenly back to pissed-off. I need to squash this if people are beginning to notice. "Get her in here," I snap, opening my office door. "I'll sort it."

After another ten minutes and a no-show from Mae, I yell for Queenie. She pops her head in the doorway, and I growl, "Where is she?"

"I dunno, Pres. I told her you wanted to see her."

"Tell her again," I snap, "and tell her if she doesn't come this time, I'm coming to get her myself." Queenie raises her eyebrows and then disappears.

Two minutes later, Dodge gets out of his basket and wags his tail. It's a tell-tale sign that Mae has arrived, and sure enough, she steps into my office. Dodge jumps up at her, licking her hands happily. "Close the door," I say firmly. She kicks it closed, and her show of disrespect pisses me off.

"Make it quick, I have a lunch date," she mutters.

NICOLA JANE

The news surprises me. Mae never really goes out with men, and I feel a slight twist in my gut. "I'll take as long as I damn well please. You need to sort the attitude out, Mae, others are noticing."

"Okay." She sighs, her tone bored.

"Mae!" I snap. She looks at me, her eyes angry. "Stop this, it's not like you."

"I'm doing what all the girls my age do, Ace. I'm getting out there, dating."

I roll my eyes. "Go on your date, Mae. Get fucking laid. It might cheer you the fuck up."

"Yes, sir," she snaps, saluting me and spinning on her heel. I don't like this side of her, and as she leaves, I breathe a sigh of relief. If she carries on, I'll speak to her mum, Bernie. She and Mae are close, she'll sort her out.

I spend the next few hours making calls and checking on a few shipments I have coming in, but at the back of my mind is Mae and her date. What if it's the guy from last night at the wedding? What if she gets hurt trying to get

ACE

over me? I tap my pen on the desk, thinking up all kinds of crazy scenarios, when Hulk stomps in and flops down on the chair in front of my desk.

"What's wrong with your miserable face?" he asks, patting Dodge as he nuzzles his head onto Hulk's knee for attention.

"Do you know who Mae went on a date with?"

"I'm glad I'm not the only one who think it's weird," he says, sounding relieved. "She never goes on dates, but, man, did she look hot. If she dressed like that all the time, she'd have a lot of dates. Scar was just saying how she's been like a caterpillar in this place, and now, all of a sudden, it's like she's been set free and she's turned into this beautiful butterfly. Where was she hiding those tits?" He's so busy rambling on that he doesn't notice me grip the desk as he giving his assessment of her body. *What the hell is wrong with me?*

"I asked who she went out with, Hulk," I growl, and he stops talking and thinks for a second.

"I dunno who he is, Pres. But she's back now. She's in the bar."

NICOLA JANE

I stand, Dodge joining me, and take a walk through to the bar. I heard Mae laughing the second I left my office. She's sitting at a table with a guy I haven't seen around here before. After asking Bear for a whiskey, I tip my glass in their direction and question, "Who's the guy?"

"Mae never said. You want me to go and ask?" I shake my head.

"He seem legit to you?"

"Erm, I guess. I didn't really speak with him, Pres. He's making her smile, which is nice to see." Somehow, that just pisses me off more.

Dodge makes his way over to them, and Mae strokes him. I hear her tell the guy about Dodge and how I found him. The guy tries to stroke him too, but the faithful mutt growls, forcing the guy to retreat his hand and they share another laugh. I whistle, calling Dodge back to my side. I lock eyes with Mae, and something pulls in my chest. I want it to go back to how it was before she told me, because right now, we feel a million miles apart . . . and I hate it.

MAE

ACE

Lee has been asking me for a date since, well, I don't even remember, it's been so long. When I began working in the office at the garage, Lee was one of the mechanics. He's since left, but we kept in touch. And now things are out in the open with Ace and I've made a complete idiot of myself, I've decided to move forward. He's made himself very clear.

"I was surprised when I got your text," says Lee. "I must've asked you out a hundred times or more." He smiles, and I blush. "Is he your dad?" I glance in the direction of where Ace is. He's leaning against the bar, staring at the big screen television and occasionally glancing in our direction.

"No, my dad's dead. But he's the President of The Rebellion MC."

"I heard some stories about the MC. Bunch of criminals, dealing in drugs?"

"You should never listen to stories, especially far-fetched ones like that." It's something you get used to, defending the club. People always focus on negative stories, but in truth, the MC brings a lot to the local area. They raise money for deprived families, help feed the homeless on cold nights, and they take Christmas presents to children in the hospital. But it doesn't matter what you say to some people, they'll believe what they want to believe. It makes dating outside the club so much harder.

"Well, he doesn't look too pleased about me being here," says Lee.

"He's just having a bad day, I imagine. He has a lot on his shoulders. He isn't bothered about me, so I wouldn't take it personal."

The rest of the date is awkward and conversation is stilted. It doesn't help that Ace is staring over at us, making us both feel uncomfortable. It eventually comes to an end, and Lee kisses me on the cheek before promising to call me in a few days, but I don't hold out much hope.

"Good date?" quips Ace as I pass him.

"Why are you watching me? It's a little weird."

"I'm not watching you, Mae. I'm just having a drink and watching football," he snaps. I roll my eyes and head for the kitchen. I don't understand him, and he never watches football.

ACE

My mum looks up from where she's chopping vegetables. "Veggies?" I ask, screwing my nose up. The guys never eat vegetables.

Mum looks guilty. "Don't tell a soul that you saw me chopping these," she says, pointing the knife at me. I take a step back and laugh at her serious face.

"Okay," I say slowly, "what's the deal with them?"

"I always hide them in their food, okay. Today is pie day, so I'm going to blend these up and put them in the gravy."

"Oh my god, Mum, you seriously go to all this trouble?"

"Everyone needs fruit and veggies, sweetie. These guys stay strong through my secret recipes, which contain these." She smirks, holding up a carrot.

Piper marches into the kitchen with Hulk hot on her heels. Mum innocently lays a clean dish towel over her secret ingredients and goes about washing the dishes. "Who the fuck is he?" he growls, slamming his hand against the wall.

"I'm not going to tell you, no matter how many walls you hit," she snaps.

"We'll see about that," he yells, stomping out of the kitchen and slamming the door behind him.

"What the hell was that?" I ask as Piper pulls herself up onto the counter.

She sighs. "That was Hulk's way of telling me he's jealous."

"If he gets so jealous, why doesn't he just commit to you?"

"I have no idea, Mae. He has no idea. I'm sick of him. So, you're hot gossip around here today. Who was the date with?"

My mum looks over in surprise. "You had a date? Why am I only just hearing about it?"

I shake my head. "Don't even go there, it was a huge mistake."

"I'm just pleased to see you getting yourself out there," Mum says, smiling.

I sigh. "Don't get too excited. I really don't think dating is for me."

"You know what you need, right?" asks Piper. "You need a makeover."

ACE

"Oh no, I really don't." I've been on the receiving end of one of Piper's makeovers before. It ended in a messy night out and some bad choices on my part.

"Please, it'll cheer us both up. We could hit the town tonight." The thought of going out for a few drinks with the girls does sound appealing. Piper sees me wavering and jumps down from the worktop. "Yay," she squeals excitedly. "Let's go."

Chapter Four

ACE

I lay my playing cards out on the table, and Scar groans as I pull the pile of cash towards me. "I'm done," he says, sighing and chucking his own cards on the table in defeat.

"Be thankful we didn't put our bikes down like you wanted to," I say with a laugh. He always takes it a step further than just cash, but tonight, I wasn't in the mood. "You'll never meet a woman if you keep wasting your money, Scar," I advise, not that he'll listen to the friendly advice.

"Pres, Angel's here," he mutters, keeping his voice low. I spot her enter the bar. Her hot pants don't leave much to the imagination and her tits are practically spilling out over her top. "Man, she looks hot tonight," he adds with a grin.

I tap him upside the head. "Show some respect," I growl.

"You made the rules, Pres. Club whores are a free-for-all unless you claim them," says Hulk, sinking down into the seat beside me.

"Don't mean you can't be respectful," I grumble.

Scar's mouth falls open. "Well, shit," he mutters. We turn to see what's caught his attention, and I stand abruptly, knocking my chair to the floor at the sight of Mae and Piper. Hulk drinks his whiskey down in one go and slams his glass on the table. He clearly isn't happy with Piper's short dress and high boots.

"She looks like a damn hooker," Hulk growls.

My eyes are stuck on Mae, so I don't really pay much attention to Piper's outfit. Her waist-length hair is usually tied up, but tonight, it flows in loose waves down her back. She's wearing tight black leather pants that show off her rounded arse perfectly and a low-cut black vest. Her black heeled boots alter her posture, making her look more confident, but it's her face that has me transfixed. The smoky eyes, the red lips . . . she looks hot. Mae catches me staring, and I look away quickly, sitting back down and gulping my drink.

"Shit, look at Mae. She looks beautiful," says Scar.

"She scrubs up well," Hulk agrees.

"I might get her a drink," says Scar, rushing off towards the girls. I press my lips together, making sure I don't do anything stupid, like tell Scar to sit his arse down and stay the hell away from Mae.

"What's up with you?" asks Hulk. "You and Mae seem off-kilter."

"Yeah, we had a disagreement."

"About?" he probes, and I take a minute to think it through before eventually deciding to speak the truth. After all, Hulk is my Vice President and my son, though we're more like best friends.

"She told me something and it knocked me for six, man," I begin. "She likes me."

Hulk's eyes widen in shock. "No fucking way," he gasps. I nod to confirm it. "But she's younger than me!"

"I know, right. I didn't see it coming," I admit.

ACE

"What did you say?"

"That it could never happen, that I was too old for her."

Hulk smirks. "I bet you're regretting that decision tonight."

"Shut up, man. I don't see her like that."

"You can have your pick of the girls, Pops. No one's gonna judge. No one would dare."

Scar sits back down. "She said she'd go on a date with me." He looks as shocked as we do.

"What the fuck? You never showed interest in Mae," says Hulk, stealing the words right out of my mouth.

"Yeah, well, Mae didn't ever look like that before. She's been hiding herself away under those baggy shirts of hers."

"You don't stand a chance, brother. Sorry to break it to yah, but she has the hots for someone older," says Hulk, slapping Scar on the back. I glare at him, but he doesn't take any notice. Instead, he leans closer to Scar. "She likes the Pres."

Scar raises his eyebrows. "Don't yah think you're a bit old for her, Pres?"

"I know I am, shithead, nobody said I liked her back," I snap. "And you need to keep your mouth shut," I add, pointing to Hulk.

"You didn't say it was a secret."

Angel sits herself in my lap, wrapping her arm around my shoulder. "What's the secret?" she asks.

Scar smirks. "That Pres has an admirer."

"Competition, I like it," she says seductively. "Who is she?"

"We can't say." Hulk shrugs but nods towards the girls.

Angel smiles wide and turns to look at me. "Please don't tell me little miss square is having dirty dreams about the big bad President." The guys crack up, clearly amused by Angel's nasty tongue. "She'd never be able to handle you. Isn't she still a virgin?"

"I heard not," says Scar.

I know she's not a virgin, but not because we talked about that shit. I mean, we were close but not that close. I overheard her a few years ago, telling Piper, and it sounded like she'd hated every second of it. "It's all a bit much, though, just to hang around the bar," says Angel, watching the girls laugh and dance around.

"They're going out. They're just waiting for Lucy and her friends to text them to meet up," says Scar.

Hulk looks annoyed. "Where are they going?"

"To one of the nightclubs that Tag owns. Apparently, he doesn't let Lucy out of his sight, so he'll be around there too."

"Maybe we should go," suggests Hulk.

I sigh. "Count me out." I know forty isn't old, but I've long stopped going to nightclubs.

"We can get into the VIP area. Lucy would love to see us," argues Hulk.

"That sounds so good." Angel smiles. "Let's go."

I shake my head. "You guys go, have a great time."

"You're showing your age," says Hulk. "Come join your kids on a night out."

Angel leans in close, pressing a kiss to my cheek. "I'll treat you," she whispers, smiling sweetly. It gets my interest, and she grinds her backside against my cock. "I love to fuck in public."

NICOLA JANE

I stand, placing her on her feet. "Let's go," I say suddenly. Angel laughs, and the guys look at me confused. "But make Bear come, so I'm not the oldest one there."

MAE

I feel great about myself. Having Piper help me get ready tonight was a game changer. She didn't push me too far out of my comfort zone, but it was enough to help me feel confident and beautiful. And now, somehow, our girly night has turned into a Rebellion night out.

Lucy's husband, Tag, owns this nightclub, so we get VIP treatment whenever we come. It's the first time Ace has ever been out with us to a club, but I'm not foolish enough to think it's because of me, seeing as Angel told us she'd promised him risky sex. I can't pretend it didn't bother me, but I do my best to plaster on a fake smile and pretend everything is fine.

"You look sad again, Mae," groans Piper, and I instantly feel bad. I thought my acting skills were better.

"I'm fine, Pip, sorry," I say, rubbing her arm and smiling.

"Who is it? Who's this guy you're upset about?"

ACE

"It's not important," I say firmly. "I've decided to put all that behind me and move forward."

"We just want to see you happy again."

Lucy dances over, wiggling her backside. Tag is two steps behind her, scowling. He places his hands on her hips to still them and growls something in her ear. She laughs and then takes a seat next to me. "I'm going to see Ace. Be good," Tag warns before walking away.

"He's so hot," groans Piper.

"He's so intense," I say.

Lucy grins, glancing back at where her husband is talking to Ace. "I'm so lucky." We fall about making vomit noises and pretending to stick our fingers down her throat. She giggles. "Distract me with gossip."

"Scar asked me on a date earlier," I announce.

"I thought he liked Nova," says Piper. "You go from no dates to two in one day."

"What's going on with you?" asks Lucy. "Why the sudden urge to get yourself out there?"

NICOLA JANE

I shrug. "Seeing you getting married and settling, everyone else seems to be attached to someone, I don't know, I guess I'm sick of being on my own."

"It's about time, if you ask me," says Piper.

I spot Ace and Angel moving towards the roof terrace. A jealousy burns through me, and before I can talk myself out of it, I'm on my feet. "I need to pee," I say, excusing myself from the table. I have no idea what I'm going to do, I just know I can't sit by, knowing they're out there having sex. Even as I follow them, I'm trying to convince myself it's a stupid move. Outside, the air is fresh, and I shiver. Piper wouldn't let me wear a jacket because it didn't go with the outfit.

Ace has his strong, tattooed arms wrapped around Angel, and they're both peering over the wall, looking down on the street below. He looks back at me. "Mae," he says, looking concerned. He straightens up and moves towards me. "Everything okay?"

I nod. "I needed some air," I say, smiling. "Sorry, I didn't know you were both out here."

ACE

"Join us," he offers, and I'm relieved he's acting like normal.

Angels laughs. "Are you serious right now?"

Ace looks back at her. "Stop," he says, his tone warning.

She rolls her eyes. "Fine, I'll leave you two *alone*," she mutters, heading back inside.

I wait until she's gone and smile. "Sorry, I just wanted air."

"Don't mind her." Ace shrugs out of his jacket and then places it around my shoulders. "You're cold."

"Piper said I couldn't wear a jacket cos it messed up the outfit," I explain.

He grins. "Well, you look great. I was hoping to get a minute alone with you tonight."

My heart dances with joy as he points me in the direction of the seating area. Once we're sitting down, he smiles awkwardly. "I hate that we're fighting. I've handled this all wrong. I shouldn't have gotten mad at you for being honest. You can't help your feelings, and I'm flattered, I really am."

"But?" I ask, because I know there is one.

"But . . . I'm not good enough for you. I'm all kinds of bad, Mae. The shit I've done haunts me at night. You should be with a decent man, one who's as good inside as you."

I give a small smile. "I'll work my way through the line of men just waiting to take me out," I joke.

He smiles too. "You're too guarded, Mae. You don't put yourself out there enough."

"I know. I'm gonna try harder."

Ace places a finger under my chin and lifts my face to look at his. His bright blue eyes send shivers down my spine. "You won't be single for long, not once you start looking. I wish things could be different, and if I were a few years younger . . ." He sighs. "Sorry."

I nod sadly, forcing another smile. "Thanks for clearing the air. I promise not to lay any more kisses on you."

I expect him to laugh too, but he's staring intently at my mouth, like he's lost in thought. There's conflict in his eyes, like he's at war with himself, and then he moves closer, just a fraction. I hold my breath, not daring to believe he might kiss me. I daren't make a sound as he moves closer still, until he's a breath away. Finally, his lips gently press against mine for a brief second, then his brow furrows and he tilts his head slightly to swipe his tongue against my lips. Instinctively, I open for him, and Ace doesn't hesitate to close his mouth over mine in a hungry kiss. I feel lightheaded as his hands move to either side of my face, settling in my hair and tugging gently at the roots. It feels so good, I curl my toes.

Ace begins to stand, pulling me with him and keeping our mouths joined. He walks me backwards until I hit the wall. Standing with him towering over me like this is a huge turn-on. He keeps one hand tangled in my hair as the other travels down my body, his fingers lightly stroking along my ribs until he gets to my arse. Cupping a handful of flesh, he gently pulls me closer to him until I feel his erection between our bodies.

Suddenly, Ace pulls away, panting. His eyes dart around like a wild animal looking for an escape. "Shit," he mutters.

I don't want to give him a chance to reject me, and I know it's coming just by the regret written all over his face.

NICOLA JANE

I stand on my tiptoes and place a gentle kiss on his cheek, and then I turn away and head back inside.

I head straight to the girls, feeling a little smug as I pass the table where Angel is sitting with Scar. I'm about to take a seat when Angel shouts my name. I roll my eyes, and Piper pats my hand. "Don't bite," she whispers as I turn to face her.

"You seem awfully happy for someone who just got rejected," she says. Scar mutters something in her ear, and she scowls at him. Club girls shouldn't mouth off to members or their family, and I'm sure he's relaying that reminder.

I arch a brow. "Rejected?" I repeat, smirking. *If only she knew.*

"That's why I gave you space, so he could put an end to your stupid little crush." She gives a laugh. "I mean, seriously, do you honestly think a man like him, the club President, would look at you? Aren't you still a virgin?" She laughs again.

"Shut the fuck up, Angel," Piper snaps. "The Pres will go mental when he hears you talking to a club family member like this."

"I doubt it. One day, I'll be his old lady, then I can talk any way I want to."

"Mae's right, Angel," says Scar. "Shut the hell up. You ain't an old lady yet."

I listen to their exchange feeling mortified, all the while wondering where the hell she's heard all this. Would Ace really tell her what happened between us?

"I'm just being straight with her," Angel defends. "Ace is too nice to say it, but I'm not. Back the fuck off because he isn't into you like that. He's old enough to be your dad."

I take a steadying breath, realising the only way to face this humiliation is to deny everything. "What are you talking about?" I ask. "I'm not into him like that. We're friends."

"Cut the crap. We know," says Angel, laughing harder. "We know you have a crush on him. He told us."

"Angel, I swear to god, Pres is gonna kill you for this," snaps Scar.

I can't stop the redness warming my cheeks as I'm hit with embarrassment. I look around at the girls, then to Scar. "Is she right? Did he tell everyone?"

NICOLA JANE

"No," says Scar, rushing towards me. "He wouldn't do that—"

I can't listen to him lie, so I rush off in the direction of the bathroom, jumping the queue while muttering an apology, and locking myself in a cubicle. Humiliation hits me hard, and I lean over the toilet, retching. Tears burn my eyes. *I can't believe he's done this to me.*

Chapter Five

ACE

I lean against the wall, watching the street below me. What the fuck did I just do? One minute, I'm talking to Mae, and the next, I have my tongue down her throat. I groan, burying my face in my hands. I've never looked at Mae like I did tonight, and I don't know if I have the makeover to thank for that, or the fact that I now know how she feels. Either way, I'm screwed. I push myself off the wall and head back inside. I'll figure it out.

I see Mae rushing towards the bathroom looking upset. Scar is about to follow her, but Angel grabs his arm to stop him. I groan again—this can't be good.

NICOLA JANE

"What happened?" I ask as I approach them from behind. They both jump, and Angel smirks. Scar glares at her, arching a brow. "Start talking, Angel."

"I told her straight, you're not interested in little girls."

"You did what?" I growl.

"In front of us all," Piper chips in.

Rage fills me. "Why the fuck would you do that?"

"I did you a favour," Angel argues, looking outraged.

"It wasn't your place. You're a fucking club whore."

"Who sleeps in your bed," she reminds me. "I have a right to tell the bitch to back off."

I step forward, but Scar holds me back. "Don't, Pres, she ain't worth it."

I take a calming breath. "Get the fuck out of my face, Angel. I'm about to break my number one rule," I growl. "And don't be in my fucking bed when I get home."

She rolls her eyes and grabs her bag. "Whatever."

"I tried to stop her, Pres. She runs her mouth wider than she spreads her legs," explains Scar as we watch her leave.

"I'd better go and smooth things with Mae." I sigh. "Was she okay?"

ACE

Scar winces and shakes his head. "It was pretty humiliating for her. Actually, can I ask you something?" I nod. "I just wanna check there's nothing between you two. I asked her on a date and all, and I don't wanna step on your toes."

I laugh, ignoring the twist inside, and pat him on the shoulder. "Firstly, you couldn't step on my toes cos I'd chop your damn feet off. And secondly, Mae is a friend, part of my club. But not my old lady and far too young for me."

The bathroom is busy. As I step inside, a few of the girls waiting bat their lashes and smile suggestively. "Mae," I growl, ignoring them, but she doesn't answer. "Mae, get out here or I'm coming in to get you."

"I'll be a minute or two," mumbles Mae, trying to sound fine, but I swear she's crying. It twists my heart, knowing it's because of me.

"I'm counting. Five, four, three . . ."

"Damn it, Ace, give me five minutes!" she yells from behind the second stall. I apologise to the ladies waiting before lifting my heavy boot and kicking the door. It pops open, and Mae looks up in surprise.

"Two, one," I finish with a smirk. "Let's go."

She glares at me, and fuck, if she's not angry. I've never seen this side of her. She's the one who soothes drama with her calming words and level head. Right now, she's anything but. "Get. Out." Each word sounds like a growl, and I wonder where she's been hiding this side of herself. She stands and moves a step closer. "How dare you humiliate me like that?" The chatter in the bathroom dies down, and I glance around at the curious faces now watching our exchange. Mae seems oblivious as she shoves me harder in the chest. "You told me nothing could happen, and I accepted that, but then you go and throw in that toe-curling kiss like something could happen—"

I smirk. "Toe-curling?"

Another shove backs me against the wash basins. "But all along, you were laughing at me behind my back. Telling everyone."

ACE

Our audience gasps, and I roll my eyes at their dramatics. "Seriously, ladies," I say, glancing around the room, "it wasn't like that."

"I've been there for you and never told a soul anything we've discussed. I keep all your little secrets because I thought we were friends and that's what friends do."

She pushes me one last time, but this time, I grab her wrists. "Careful, Mae. Remember who the fuck I am," I warn.

She scoffs, pulling free. "Yeah, pull the president card now, Ace. You're still a prick." I watch her storm from the bathroom.

"Show's over," I mutter to the women still watching me with interest.

"You better think of a good grovel," one comments, "cos she ain't happy with you."

Like I don't fucking know. I follow after Mae, shaking my head in frustration. This is just one of the reasons I don't date. I always fuck it up somehow and then I have to deal with the drama that follows. I don't have time for any of it.

NICOLA JANE

I spot Hulk looking just as pissed-off as me. "You seen Mae?" I shout over the music. Hulk nods in the direction of the dance floor, and I see why he looks so pissed. Piper, Mae, and some of the other women are dancing with a group of men. "I need a drink," I tell him, patting him on the shoulder.

Sitting back at our table, I pour myself a whiskey. Give me a quiet bar full of my men over this bullshit any day. Hulk joins me, looking tormented. "Ignore her. She wants a reaction from you."

"She's gonna get one if she touches that guy's muscles again," he growls.

"You know, you can stop all this by just claiming her," I suggest, but I already know the response. He takes after me. He doesn't want to settle down, and who can blame him? He grew up listening to the raging arguments between me and his mum.

"Not an option," he mutters.

"Then you gotta let her go. She ain't gonna save herself in the hope you might want her."

ACE

"Why can't it just stay how it is? We have a good time together, so why's she gotta be all over other men?"

I shrug. "Women want to feel like the centre of your world. What you two have is sex, but she wants her forever. If that ain't with you, you gotta leave her alone to move on." I drink some of my whiskey before setting the glass back down. "I kissed Mae," I confess.

I feel his eyes burning into me. "You did what?"

"I know, man. As much a shock to me as you."

"And you're lecturing me on mixed signals." He smirks. "You going there with her?"

I shake my head. "Not an option," I say, using his words. "But she's upset with me right now. Angel opened her mouth, and now, Mae thinks everyone knows how she feels about me."

"She'll get over it. Avoid her for a few days, she'll soon calm down."

I finish my drink. "I guess."

We fall silent, both sitting in our misery. As I watch Mae, I notice things I've never seen before. Like the way her hips sway in time to the music, even when she's not really dancing. And how she taps her nails against her bottom teeth when she's listening to someone speaking. Then there's things I've seen before but feel different when I see them now, like how she throws her head back to laugh, or how she reaches behind her back to touch the ends of her hair, twisting it around her fingers.

The guy she's speaking to leans in closer, also touching the ends of her hair until his fingers are entwined with hers. He moves his other hand to her arse as he talks into her ear. She's smiling, and it's infectious. I feel myself smiling too, even though I don't know what the joke is.

"Let's go," snaps Hulk, standing abruptly. "I can't sit around and watch her with other men." He's talking about Piper, of course, but his words hit home as I watch the guy twist Mae's head towards him. They kiss, and my fists ball by my sides. Why the fuck did she put herself on my radar? Now, I feel this itch to protect her, even from men she wants to kiss.

ACE

We get back to the clubhouse, and Hulk goes straight up to bed in a mood. I drink a few shots alone, but even the alcohol does nothing to stop me thinking about Mae. It's frustrating.

I wander around the club. It's quiet tonight, and I hate it quiet, preferring it full and buzzing to life. I stop outside Mae's bedroom door. Maybe I should wait up for her, to make sure she's home safe. I shake my head—that's ridiculous, she's a grown woman. I turn to walk away and then change my mind again, deciding I can wait and smooth things out with her. Before I know it, I'm in her room and settled in her reading chair with just her damn twinkling lights illuminating the room.

It's almost an hour later when I hear giggling from outside the room. I impatiently tap my fingers on the arms of the chair. The door opens and she practically falls through it laughing, followed by the guy she kissed earlier tonight. I grip the arms of the chair tighter, digging my fingers into the worn leather. "Get naked," he orders, and she giggles again.

"So bossy," she swoons, and I roll my eyes. *She hasn't seen bossy yet.*

"Come on, baby, stop teasing me," the guy pants out, like a dog on heat. Fuck, he's like a horny teenager.

"I'll get something for you to tie me up with," she suggests excitedly, and this surprises me. My little admirer likes a bit of mild kink. Mae holds up a rope from her dressing gown, and I shake my head. If he uses that, he's an amateur. He takes it, just like I knew he would.

Mae lies on the bed and lets him tie her hands together before securing them to the bars of her headboard. He leans over her, moving his clumsy fingers to her top. "I wouldn't do that if I was you," I growl, and they both turn in fright to look at me.

"Shit," shouts the guy, stepping back from Mae, and holding up his hands. "Is that your dad?"

"Fuck, Ace, what the hell are you doing?" snaps Mae, tugging on her restraints. "Let me out of these," she adds, glaring at the guy.

He moves towards her, and I stand abruptly, so he freezes. "Get out," I murmur. He gives Mae an uncertain look. "Didn't you hear me?" I ask with more force in my tone.

Mae sighs. "It's fine. You'd better go. I'll call you."

"You won't," I say, folding my arms over my chest and glaring at him. He backs out the room, feeling along the wall behind him for the exit and practically running out.

I slam the door closed and flick the lock, then walk back over to the chair while shrugging off my kutte. I place it over the back, taking my gun from my waistband and laying it on the bedside table. I feel her eyes following me as I move around the room. "Let me out of this," she snaps, tugging her hands.

"Did you even get his name?" I ask, staring down at her. "You let a stranger tie you up. He could have done anything to you."

She smirks. "Kinda the point."

"He was an amateur. He wouldn't have made you come, Mae," I murmur, unclipping my belt.

Her eyes dart to my hands as she bites her lower lip. "Well, I guess I'll never know, will I."

NICOLA JANE

I rip my belt from the loops, and she inhales sharply. Seeing her vulnerable broke my final straw. I have no resolve left. "I'm gonna fuck you, Mae. Show you what it feels like to have a real man make you come."

"You are?" she asks, her voice coming out breathless.

I nod, dragging my finger along her leg. "I'm gonna untie you because I don't fuck women who use fluffy pink robe ties as restraints." I smirk. "Keep your hands above your head." I continue dragging my finger along her body, pulling her top with it and exposing her lace bra. I make quick work of removing the robe tie, dropping it to the floor, and I hold up my belt, silently asking for permission. She nods, and I wrap the belt around one wrist and pull it through the metal of her bed. I then wrap it around the second wrist and secure it. I tug it to show her how secure it is. "You wanna come out of this, you just say the word." She nods again.

I stare down at her for a few seconds, ignoring the warning voice in my head telling me this will change everything. I push her top farther up her body. "What have you done to me, Mae?" Tugging the cups of her bra down, I groan

ACE

at the sight of her perfect breasts. "We're about to cross a line," I add. She nods, keeping her eyes fixed on me. Her breathing is coming in fast bursts, making her chest rise and fall. I lean closer, flicking my tongue over a pert nipple, and she hisses. "Let's hope we can survive it," I whisper.

MAE

I close my eyes in pleasure. His mouth is the only part of his body touching me, and as he pays attention to my other nipple, I twist my body closer to him, needing more. He steps back and my eyes shoot open. He smirks. "I gotta grab something from my room. Stay still." He backs out the room, leaving the door open. I glare after him, aware someone could walk past any second and see me like this.

A few minutes pass and I'm beginning to panic, but then I finally hear footsteps and he appears by the door. "Pres," shouts Bear, and my eyes widen in panic. Ace gives me an easy grin.

"Yeah?" he replies.

"Are you coming down for a game of poker?"

"I'd love to Bear," he pauses, glancing at me again with another smirk, "but yah know what, I promised Bernie I'd have a chat with Mae about her crazy moods lately. Maybe I'll join you when I'm done."

"Okay, Pres, your call, but Scar is so drunk right now and he's betting crazy money."

Ace laughs. "It's tempting. Let me see how this goes first." He steps into the room and locks the door again. "You almost got caught," he says, looking amused. "I bet if I checked, you'd be wet for me, Mae."

His deep, gravelly voice and his dirty words cause me to rub my thighs together to get some kind of friction. There's an ache where I need him to be right now, but he doesn't seem to be in any rush.

"Patience," he whispers, reading my body language. He holds up a blindfold. "I wanna tease you first, Mae."

I nod, and he ties the blindfold in place. I've not had a very adventurous sex life, but being tied up and blindfolded is at the top of my to-do list. He runs something soft over my breast, circling my nipple. "Why did you tell me, Mae? Things were simpler before I knew." His fingers work the button on my trousers, then he tugs them down my legs and discards them. The feathery touch returns, running up my leg and over my stomach. "I already got my seat reserved in hell," he adds, "and you're determined to send me lower with a first-class ticket."

The bed dips and I feel him over me, his legs either side of me before he takes a nipple into his mouth. I arch my back off the bed, and his hands run down my sides until he's cupping my arse. He works his mouth down my body and over my stomach. I hold my breath in anticipation. I've never had a man go down on me before, but something tells me I'm about to experience my first time with Ace.

Chapter Six

ACE

I should be talking myself out of this, but as I move my mouth down her body, tasting every inch of her soft skin, all thoughts of stopping are gone. I squeeze her arse, lifting her to my waiting mouth and pressing it over her pussy. She cries out in surprise, gripping the leather belt and tugging. "Jesus," she hisses. I work my tongue through her folds, lapping up her juices and humming my approval. She writhes around in pleasure, small breathy sounds escaping every so often which only spur me on. "You ever had a man eat your pussy before Mae?" I growl. She shakes her head, and it gives me pleasure knowing I'm the first to give her this.

ACE

When I feel her begin to shake, her orgasm pending, I pull away, kneeling up and popping the button on my jeans. I take the condom from my back pocket and rip it open. "You okay with this?" I growl. "Because if you don't want this to go further, then say so now, Mae. I don't know if I can stop myself once I'm inside you."

"I want this," she says, her voice husky.

I take my shaft, moving my hand along it once and wiping the bead of pre-cum from the end onto my thumb. I press my thumb against her lips, and her tongue darts out, licking it clean.

I line myself up, ignoring the small voice in the back of my head telling me this is a huge mistake. I need her . . . I need this. I inch into her slowly until I'm as far as she can take me. I unfasten the belt holding her wrists, wanting her hands on my skin. This is more than a casual fuck—there's a connection, I felt it the second I touched her. She immediately reaches for my face and tugs me down until our mouths clash together in a hungry kiss. Her legs wrap around my thighs, and I begin to move. I try to go easy, but she feels too good, and my body takes over, fucking her until she's sliding up the bed. She grips my shoulders, her nails marking my skin. The pain only adds to my excitement as I chase my release.

I take Mae's hand and guide it between our sweaty bodies, leaning back slightly so I can watch her touch herself. She begins to shudder, and I knock her hand out the way, wanting to feel her orgasm on my cock. I slam into her over and over, growling as she comes apart, clenching me inside her. I follow seconds later, unable to control it any longer.

I fall over her, keeping my weight on my elbows but burying my face into her shoulder. "Fuck," I pant against her clammy skin. "That shit was hot."

Mae lays silent, running her fingers through my hair. Doubt suddenly creeps in, wondering if she's regretting it. I roll off her, laying by her side. "You okay, Mae?" I ask, unfastening the blindfold.

She blinks a few times, then turns her head to look at me. Her cheeks are slightly pink, and her lips are swollen from our kisses. She looks beautiful. "I'm scared you'll run any minute," she admits.

ACE

I trace my finger over her collar bone. "I couldn't run even if I wanted to. Whatever just happened between us felt right, Mae, like it was always meant to be."

She suppresses a smile. "Really?"

"I can't let you walk away. Somehow, we have to come up with a plan. One that keeps you safe but means we can do this a lot more."

"Keeps me safe?"

"You know I avoid relationships for a reason. I may as well just paint a bullseye on your backside," I mutter.

We fall silent, and I pull her closer until her leg is wrapped over my own and her head is on my chest. It's not enough, I need more so I pull her to lay over me. "I used to have a reoccurring nightmare that I'd fall in love and some fucker would slit her throat. I don't know what I'd do if something bad happened to you because of me."

"So, what happens now?" she asks sleepily.

"Sleep. Let me worry about it." I place a chaste kiss on her head and wrap her in my arms. It feels good to have her with me, and I find my eyes growing heavier with each breath.

MAE

I wake feeling far too hot. I'm surprised to find Ace still wrapped around me, and my heart does a little happy dance. His words last night gave me comfort because I was fully prepared for him to use me and walk away, and I felt okay with that. I just needed to know what it was like to be with him. And the risk paid off because he wants more.

There's a scratching at my bedroom door, and I hear Dodge whimpering. He must know his master is in here. I extract myself expertly from Ace's strong hold and creep across to open the door. Dodge rushes in, diving onto the bed and licking Ace's face. He splutters, pushing Dodge away but instantly smiling at his best friend. "You need to stop stalking me, you'll give the game away." He ruffles the dog's fur, and Dodge lays down beside him, finally pleased to be next to his master again.

"So, did you figure it out?" I ask.

Ace looks to the clock and sits up suddenly, taking the dog by surprise. "Shit, is that the time?" I glance at the clock and see it's ten a.m. Usually, I'm awake at the crack

ACE

of dawn for my run, so I'm just as shocked. He jumps out of bed and begins hopping around to pull his clothes on. "Fuck, I have a meeting with Tag."

"Can't you call and cancel?"

"No, it's important. Club business." He runs his fingers through his hair, "I never sleep in. I always wake after three or four hours of sleep." He looks confused and uncomfortable. I watch as he passes me, heading for the door.

A panic fills me, and I begin to think this is an excuse to run out on me. Maybe he's changed his mind. He pulls the door open and turns back. "Stop overthinking, Mae. Nothing's changed. What I said last night, stands. I'm gonna find a way to keep you."

I smile while I shower and dress, hardly believing my dreams are coming true. I head down to the kitchen to see if Mum's saved any breakfast leftovers. She's sitting at the kitchen table with Queenie, their heads together like a pair of old wives plotting. "Good morning. You're late waking up today," states Queenie suspiciously.

I feel a blush creep on my cheeks and turn towards the fridge to avoid them spotting it. "Yeah, it was a late night."

NICOLA JANE

"Ah," says Mum, "so you went out?"

I pull out a cold sausage. "Yeah."

"You meet anyone?" asks Queenie, and I panic. My brain goes into overdrive, and I almost choke my answer out while cramming the sausage into my mouth. "Sort of, why?"

"Just something Scar mentioned over breakfast. Says he caught a guy sneaking outta here late last night while the guys were playing poker. Almost shot the poor guy."

I spin to face them, mid-chew. "He didn't, though, right?" I feel bad enough that Ace kicked him outta here like that without him getting hurt because of me.

"No, but Scar was pissed you kicked him out like that and didn't escort him out the clubhouse. What if he'd have been someone out to get The Rebellion? You could've put everyone in danger. I think he might speak to Pres about it, Mae, so be prepared for—" Queenie is cut off before she can finish.

Ace's voice rings out through the building, his tone angry. "Mae!" he yells. "Mae, get the fuck out here!" I jump in fright.

ACE

My mum stands, looking panicked. "Don't get smart with him, Mae. Just take the yelling and apologise. You know how moody he is lately," she hisses. I nod, not knowing what the fuck to expect.

Ace shoves the door open, banging it against the wall, and I jump in fright. His eyes fall to me, and I notice Scar and Hulk behind him looking just as pissed. "My office now," he growls.

Inside the office, all three men stare at me, and I feel the anger vibrating off the walls. "Did I do something wrong?" I almost whisper.

"You let a guy leave here last night and didn't escort him out?" asks Ace. My eyes widen. Has he seriously pulled me in here to yell at me about something he did? I catch a pleading look in his eyes, a split second of panic when he realises I may not keep his secret.

I sigh, knowing I'm going to protect him. "I was drunk," I offer feebly, "and I passed out."

"So, not only did you bring a stranger back here, but you were so drunk that you didn't even keep your wits about you? He could have been anyone, you stupid bitch," shouts Hulk.

I frown, trying to hold my own temper. "I'm sorry, okay, no need for name calling."

"Sorry isn't going to keep us fucking safe if you mess up like that again," snaps Scar.

"It won't happen again. In all these years, that's the first time I messed up," I remind him.

"It's not good enough," snaps Hulk. "You put the whole club in danger."

Ace paces the floor, running his fingers through his hair. "Tag's waiting for the meeting to start. Could you guys go ahead and start? I'll deal with Mae."

"You sure, Pres?" asks Hulk, and Ace nods, patting his son on the back.

Both men glare at me as they pass, and I almost wilt at their rage, but as soon as the door closes, I'm hauled up into Ace's arms and pushed hard against the wall. His hands pull at my clothing, lifting my top until my breast is in his mouth. His kisses are hurried and frenzied. He stands me on the ground again and tugs at my shorts, pushing them down my legs until I've stepped out of them. I watch as he fiddles around with a condom, sheathing his large erection.

"Hands against the wall," he whispers. I turn, placing my palms on the wall as instructed. I feel the head of his cock pushing at my entrance, and he gently kicks my legs farther apart, making it easier for him. He places his hand over my mouth. "Hold on, baby," he growls into my ear. "This is gonna be hard and fast."

Ace moves quickly, his pace punishing. He moves his hands to my hips, slamming into me harder. I groan, pushing my mouth against my arm to muffle the sounds. "The door isn't locked, Mae, so you need to be quicker," he warns. Panic overtakes me, followed by something else, something more like excitement, and before long, I'm shivering against him, my orgasm rushing through me, coating my legs in wetness.

Ace isn't far behind, ramming hard into me and then stilling while he empties into the condom. He waits for a few seconds, our breaths coming hard and fast, and then he pulls out of me and uses a tissue to dispose of the condom.

NICOLA JANE

He watches as I pull my clothes on. "Later, I'm gonna have you walk around my room naked," he says firmly, and another thrill shoots through me. He fastens his jeans. "But for now, I really do have a meeting to go to. Your behaviour last night is disappointing, and the men are very angry. I might have to punish you later." He smirks, and I scowl playfully. "Isn't that what that was?" I ask, pointing to the wall where he just fucked me hard and fast. He slaps me on the arse and then heads for the door. "I mean it, Mae. You won't get off so lightly next time," he yells, slamming the door in a fake temper tantrum. I smile to myself. Fake . . . I can live with that.

Chapter Seven

♥

ACE

I pause outside church to gather myself. It's a place where my men gather for meetings to discuss business or urgent situations. Some of the most important decisions are made in this room.

I shake out my shoulders and take a deep breath before entering the room with Dodge by my side. My men sit around the large table, with Tag and Anton sitting in chairs on the outside of our circle. My men belong at the table, each having earned their place here. Anton and Tag are Mafia, Anton being the head, and I trust them. They're good guys, and Tag is my son-in-law, but they haven't earned a place at my table.

NICOLA JANE

Tag called me last night to arrange this meet, saying they have news for us. I sit at the head of the table, the gavel to my right, handed down to me from my father and his father before that. I bang it once to indicate that church is now in session, and the voices around the table fall silent as all eyes turn to me. "Sorry for keeping you all waiting. Things went a little crazy."

"We heard that little Mae is going off the rails," pipes up Chuck.

"Where'd yah hear that?" I ask. "She made a small mistake. It's all sorted, no harm done." I'm playing it down because, ultimately, it was my fault. I took my eye off the ball and kicked that guy from her room without escorting him out. It was a rooky mistake because my head was too full of her.

"No harm done this time," growls Hulk. "She could have had us all killed in our beds."

"Man, if you think a little chump like that can slaughter us all in our beds then . . ." I trail off, and some of the guys around the table chuckle.

ACE

"How'd you know he was a little chump?" asks Hulk. "He could've been a seven-foot biker." I press my lips together in a fine line, realising my mistake.

"Just a guess. She looks like she goes for the geeky type."

"You're right, Pres, he was a geek." Scar smirks.

"Have we come to talk about Mae, or should we get onto real business?" I snap, my patience running thin. I can't risk talking about her or I might slip up again, and no one can know what we've done. I don't know how the guys would feel. Mae has been a part of this club since she was a small girl, raised by us all after her father was killed. "Apparently, Anton has something to tell us."

We all turn to look at Anton, who stands and straightens his expensive suit jacket. "We've had intel that Lorenzo Corallo is back in town." I grimace at this new information. Tag's father ran after he'd tried to have Tag killed so he could re-claim his title as head of the family and underboss to Anton. When the assassination failed, he went underground.

"He's using an alias, but the passport under that name was used yesterday to re-enter England."

"Do we know if he's in London?" I ask, my concern rising for my daughter and grandchild.

"I'm looking after her, Ace," snaps Tag, reading my mind.

"Where is she right now, Tag, cos I don't see her by your side?" I growl. Dodge picks up on the sudden tension in the room and stands, waiting for my instruction.

Tag gets to his feet too. "She's with my security team at the gym, and my son is with Queenie in this clubhouse. They're both safe, Ace. They're always my number one priority." Dodge grumbles, and Tag glances at him warily. I click my fingers, and he stops, choosing to sit by my feet with his eyes fixed on Tag.

"Lucy should be here, under this roof until we find him." This is the safest place for them to be right now, and Tag knows it. After he was shot, they both moved in here, but I've noticed lately they're spending more and more time at one of his places. I'm not sure Lucy even realises he's doing it, *keeping her to himself.*

"Well, you know Lucy, always challenging my decisions and pushing the boundaries," he snaps, and I wonder if everything is okay between the two. He almost sounds pissed.

"Then I suggest you get your woman in order," I hiss. "There's no way I'd have my woman out of my sight with Lorenzo around."

Anton waves his hands. "Enough! This isn't a pissing contest. I came to advise you to step up security around the club. We don't know if he knows Lucy has ties here, especially after you helped us out with him before."

When Tag was trying to help his father escape the Mafia after wronging them, we helped to pull off a fake murder, making Anton's father believe he was dead, so Tag could step into his shoes.

"Of course, it goes without saying. Tag, pull Lucy back here. I'm putting the club on lockdown." Groans erupt from around the table. "It's to keep our women safe. We don't know why he's back, or if he plans on trying to kill Tag again. We're all at risk, and most of all, so is my daughter and grandchild. I ain't risking them." I slam the gavel on the table and leave the room. I need to work off this stress, but I can't bother Mae again, she'll get sick of me.

I go to the bar, and Mae is behind it, a cloth in her hand, chatting happily to her mum. She glances in my direction, and I scowl, still playing the role of pissed-off President. "Whiskey, neat," I grumble, but she hesitates. "Which part didn't you understand?"

"Everything okay?" she asks, and I glare at her. It's something she would have asked me before we complicated everything, but I still feel like people will guess if she speaks to me like that.

"Get me the drink," I snap, and she raises her eyebrows before turning away from me and getting my drink. She slams it on the bar and the amber liquid splashes, a few drops landing on the polished wood. I'm tempted to teach her sassy mouth a lesson and have her lick the damn spill up, but she snatches the cloth from her shoulder and wipes it away.

Bernie smiles weakly. "Kids," she mutters, causing me to almost choke on my drink. It's not what I need to hear after I just fucked her against my office wall.

ACE

"We're on lockdown, Bernie," I growl, "until further notice. Spread the word and make sure the club girls are on hand for the guys. We'll all need to work off our pent-up aggression."

"You got it," says Bernie.

"Wow," huffs Mae, "work off pent-up aggression. Will *you* be doing that, Pres?" It's what I'd normally do, before her, but I can't tell her that I'll be taking my frustration out on her fine arse. Not with her mother sitting right next to me. "It's not fair on the ladies stuck here. What about me and Piper?" she goes on.

"You want me to hire male gigolos?" I offer, adding a smirk.

"Mae, please stop. What's gotten into you today?" snaps Bernie. Her mobile rings and she checks it. "That's Angel now. I'll let her know to come here."

I wait until she leaves and then I lunge forward, leaning across the bar, close to Mae's face. "Pushing your luck, baby. Keep running that smart mouth and I'll be filling it up to keep it busy." Mae's face flushes. "And for the record, you spill my whiskey again like that and I'll have you licking it up while I fuck you over this bar." I want so badly to kiss her smart mouth. She's pouting, and it's sexy as hell.

"At some point, we're gonna have to talk about what's going on, Ace. I don't want to label it or push you into anything, but I can't watch you with the club girls."

I smile. She doesn't even know that she's completely bewitched me. "There's nothing to talk about, Mae, you got me." She looks confused, but before I can clarify, Piper takes a seat next to me.

"Lockdown? What the hell, Pres? I have college."

"Speak to your tutor, get them to send work, video seminars, whatever. Just don't go sneaking off. I know what you and Lucy are like together." Since they met last year, they've become real good friends. It's nice to see and means Lucy is more likely to stick around. "No encouraging her either, Pip. This is to keep her and that little one safe."

Piper gives me her most innocent look, but I don't fall for it. She's the crazy of the kids around here. That thought sends a jolt to my heart and my eyes fall to Mae, who's wiping glasses and staring at Piper.

ACE

They're all club kids, growing up here together. It's how everyone sees them, so I can't help thinking what the hell everyone's gonna say when they find out about me and Mae. I shake the thought away. I can't worry about that shit now, not when we have Tag's father running around like a crazy idiot. But one thing I know I can't do is stop. It feels right, even though all the signs are pointing to wrong.

Mae catches my serious expression and, without words, tips her head and mouths the question, 'Are you okay?' I nod, but she doesn't look convinced. She grabs the whiskey bottle and tops up my glass, smirking and spilling extra on the bar top. I quirk my eyebrow, and she presses her lips together, stifling her grin. All kinds of images flash through my mind, mostly of her naked and me licking the amber liquid from various parts of her anatomy. "Whoops, silly me. Sorry, Pres." She lifts my glass and wipes the spillage again. "I'll pay for that later." My eyes shoot to hers in surprise, and she grins. "I have no change on me right now, but seeing as it's the second spill, I'll cover the cost of one shot."

"Don't be silly, Mae, accidents happen. I have a few jobs stacking up in my office that you can do instead. Especially if we're locked up for the next few days." I take my glass from her and head back to my office, trying to hide the smile on my face.

MAE

"Oh my god, you're fucking the Pres!" Piper whisper-hisses. My face instantly burns a deep shade of red.

"What?" I almost shout. "No, of course not. What are you talking about?"

Piper leans closer, her eyes wide. "Don't you dare lie to me, Mae Molly Grain. I've known you my whole life and I know flirting when I see it."

I try and come up with excuses, but my mind draws a blank and my mouth opens and closes like a fish. "Oh god, Pip, please don't tell anyone," I whisper.

The last thing we need right now is to be the gossip of this place. It'll spook Ace and then he'll end it. My heart can't take it when he keeps giving me hope with little hints and possessive remarks.

Piper covers her mouth. "Jesus Christ, I'm right? What the actual fuck, Mae?" she growls. "He's old."

"Not that old," I argue.

"He knew your dad."

"When you put it like that, it sounds bad, but my dad died a long time ago. I really like him, Pip. I tried not to, but I just couldn't help it."

"People used to say he had something about him that would make girls instantly fall in love, and now, one of my own girls has fallen for it. What's your mum gonna say? And what about Lucy?"

I grab hold of her hand and practically squeeze it in desperation. "Please, Piper, whatever you do, please don't tell anyone. We've barely made it to twenty-four hours, and I don't know if it's going anywhere yet, but if you tell anyone, we'll be over before we've even begun."

Piper sighs. "Okay," she mutters, "I won't tell a soul."

I sigh in relief. "Pinky promise.""Yeah, yeah." She sighs, holding out her little finger. We hook together and then smile. "Is he big?" she asks, her face serious.

I laugh, then scowl. "No dirty questions, have some respect."

"Fuck respect. If I'm keeping secrets, I want to know everything. It's the least you owe me, and I need to understand what makes you fall for a guy his age."

I laugh and grab us a bottle of wine. If we're gonna be locked up for a few days, then we may as well make the most of it.

Chapter Eight

ACE

"Pres, you might wanna get out there soon. It's getting outta hand," shouts Hulk from outside my closed office door. I chuck my pen down on the pile of papers.

"Why can't you sort it out, Hulk?"

"Because it's the women, Pres."

I roll my eyes and sigh heavily. "You pussy, get out there and sort it out. If you can't pull the women into line, then what fucking hope have you got of dealing with heavy shit? If Tag could hear you now—"

"Fuck you," he yells, cutting me off. I smile to myself. Hulk hates it when I say shit like that about Tag. Being compared to the Mafia is insulting to him.

NICOLA JANE

I groan. I was sick of going over the books anyway. I open the door, and Hulk looks surprised. "Oh, I didn't think you'd actually come out." Usually, I wouldn't, but it's been a few hours since I've seen Mae and I miss her. I sound like a pussy-whipped bitch.

I follow Hulk, with Dodge hot on my heels, into the main room. It's busy now that we're on lockdown, but because of the time, most of the kids are in bed. I spot the girls that Hulk's referring to because of the loud giggles and yelling coming from the bar area. Mae sways, a bottle of wine hanging loosely in her hand. Piper is sitting on the table, talking animatedly to her, and Lucy is watching the pair intently, her head going back and forth between them. "Well, they don't look too outta hand from here," I say.

"Man, you didn't see them on the table dancing. If they weren't part of this club, I'd have offered them all a job in the strip bar."

I raise my brows and make a mental note to get Mae to show me her moves later. Arms wrap around my neck, and from the scent of her strong, overpowering perfume, I know it's Angel before I've seen her face. We haven't spoken since she pissed me off in the nightclub, but she holds a drink out for me, which pretty much means she wants to forget the argument and move on. I take it, and she works her way around my body until she stands in front of me. Her hands rest against my chest, but I make no move to touch her back. Instead, I stare her down until she finally breaks. "Oh come on, are you still grumpy over the whole Mae thing?" I don't respond, and she reaches up and places a kiss on my cheek, "I'm sorry, Pres. Please forgive me."

"Get lost, Angel," says Hulk, scowling. "He don't want you anymore."

"What do you know?" she snaps.

"That's enough," I growl, noticing Mae's attention on us.

"Well, tell her to fuck off then. You gonna claim her and make her my step-mum? Of course, you aren't, so get rid of her."

Angel glowers at him, "You're so annoying."

NICOLA JANE

"Jesus, the pair of you are behaving like kids," I snap, removing her hands from my chest and stepping away from the two of them.

I move towards Mae. "You causing trouble in my club?" I mutter, making sure the other girls aren't paying any attention to us. "I hear you've been showing my guys what you can do."

"I was dancing. It's not my fault your guys are like dogs in heat." She quirks a brow at me. It's sexy, and I smirk.

"You can show me later, and I'll judge if it's appropriate for you to behave like that when you belong to me." I carry on towards the bar, feeling her eyes burning into the back of my head.

None of this is like me—the possessive feeling I've felt these last few days towards Mae is new to me. I liked Hulk's mum, she was strong and the type of woman who would handle a guy like me, but there was something missing between us. We didn't have that spark that made me wanna rip her clothes off and spend my days buried inside her. When she disappeared, leaving Hulk with me at just five years old, I vowed to never let a woman into our life like that again. I couldn't handle putting us through that pain a second time.

These days, with Hulk being a grown arse man, I don't have to worry about him getting attached, but I still hadn't met anyone who piqued my interest enough to want to keep them for myself. Until now. The funny thing about it is Mae's been there all along, I just didn't see it.

I end up back in my office to finish off the books, and when I resurface many hours later, the place is quiet. The main room is completely empty with the lights turned down low.

Upstairs, I head straight for Mae's bedroom. I have an idea, but I'm not sure how adventurous she is. I tap lightly on the door, and a minute later, she opens it wearing just a shirt. I take her hand, and she whispers, "Where are we going?"

"I told you what would happen if you spilled whiskey again," I say quietly.

We sneak down the stairs and into the main room. It's still dark and peaceful, much to my relief. "You can't be serious, Ace," she hisses, trying to pull free when she realises my intentions.

"Deadly." I smirk, leading her to the bar. I take down the bottle of whiskey and hand it to her. "Do it," I say, and she takes the bottle from me.

"This is crazy. What if someone catches us?" she argues.

"Pour the damn drink, Mae," I growl, then watch as she unscrews the bottle top and removes it. I unfasten my belt, and she eyes me nervously. I nod towards the bar, and she sighs before tipping some of the whiskey out onto the bar top. Without warning, I bring my hand down across her thighs, giving her a short, sharp slap. She hisses, jumping away from me.

"What the hell was that?" she growls, rubbing the sore spot. I pop the button on my jeans, smiling at her as I lower them to rest under my backside and pull out my erection. Taking her by the waist, I spin her around so her back is to me. Pulling out a silk scarf I found earlier, I place it over her mouth, tie it at the back, and then smack her arse again. This time, she jumps but doesn't make a sound. I rub the area, pushing up her nightshirt.

ACE

I step back and take in the beautiful sight before me. Her rounded ass is begging to be fucked, but for now, I settle for her wet pussy. I drag two of my fingers through her folds, and she bucks against me, groaning. "Shh, baby, you need to be quiet," I whisper.

I dip my fingers in the whiskey from the bar top and then pop them in my mouth, humming my approval. "I need to bottle that," I groan. "Your pussy and my favourite liquor, best taste ever."

I line myself up with her entrance and push straight in. Mae is shoved forward, slamming her hands onto the bar to catch herself. I feel my orgasm rushing forward, but I'm not ready to stop yet, so I pull out. I dip my hand in the whiskey again and rub it along my erection. Mae eyes me excitedly. So far, she hasn't sucked my cock, but after her behaviour tonight, she's gonna get on her knees. I pull the scarf from her mouth and pull it tight around her neck, "I'm gonna let you lick my cock, suck it like your life depends on it, Mae," I warn, and she nods eagerly.

She lowers to her knees and takes my shaft in her hands. Running her tongue over the head, she licks away the bead of pre-cum. She places her lips over the tip, and I watch in awe as she takes in my length, inch by inch. When I hit the back of her throat, she takes a breath in through her nose and pushes a little farther. The feeling is amazing, and I close my eyes in pleasure. I resist the urge to fuck her mouth, preferring to let her lead at her own pace. As she moves her head back and forth, her cheeks suck in and her head bobs up and down. I'm close, so I grip the scarf, pulling it tighter when I see her busy fingers rubbing her pussy vigorously.

A sound from the kitchen causes us both to freeze. The door opens and Hulk's shadow stumbles into the main room. I remain still, not wanting to bring his attention this way, and Mae decides it's the perfect time to run her greedy tongue down my length. I squeeze my fists into balls and bite my lip when she sucks me back into her mouth.

Hulk is stumbling towards the stairs, and I pray for him to get a move on because I feel the explosion rushing through my body. I begin to shake, my legs almost giving way, then I spill my cum into her mouth, biting so hard on my lip that I taste a tinge of blood. Mae swallows my seed while I continue to spurt into her mouth in what feels like the longest orgasm I've ever had. Hulk closes the door behind him, and I almost fall against the bar, gripping the edge to steady myself and breathing heavily.

"Fuck, Mae," I groan. She smiles up at me with an innocence that only virgins can claim. "You'll pay for that," I pant.

MAE

I never behave like this. Something about being around Ace brings out this daring, crazy person from deep inside me, and it feels exhilarating and exciting. I smile all the way back to my room, while Ace decided to stay back and clean the bar. He didn't want to risk us bumping into Hulk in case he hadn't quite stumbled into bed yet.

I shower with the same wide smile on my face and choose a silk night dress to wear for bed, a change from my usual comfortable pyjamas or T-shirts. I check my mobile and there's a text from Ace saying he's been delayed but he'll be with me shortly, so I climb into bed and settle down. I love the butterflies that dance in my stomach at the thought of being with him again. When he said I belonged to him earlier tonight, I wanted to kiss him there and then. It's the words I never expected to hear from Ace. My eyes grow heavy, and I begin to drift in and out of sleep.

Light shines onto my face, disturbing my slumber, and I stretch out and open my eyes. I know instantly that Ace isn't here, and when I glance at the clock, I'm disappointed to see it's almost nine in the morning. Ace never came to me. Whatever happened last night must have been important, and I find myself dressing quickly, hoping it isn't bad news for the club and that everyone, including Ace, is safe.

Downstairs, I find my mum in the kitchen chatting happily to Queenie. Piper is reading a newspaper at the large dinner table, and Angel is staring down at her mobile phone. "Coffee?" she asks, smiling, and I nod, taking a seat next to Piper. Nothing too bad could have happened or they wouldn't be acting so normal.

"It seems quiet in here today. Did I miss the breakfast rush?" I ask.

ACE

"A few of the guys have gone out on a run. Club business," explains Queenie. "Bear was up at the crack of dawn and woke me up. I was so annoyed."

"That explains it, Bear is out, so it's quiet," I joke, and she smiles.

"The Pres is in an awful mood today, though, so stay out of his way," my mum warns me, handing over a coffee.

Piper exchanges a smirk with me. "He's always shouting about something," she says.

"He was in a good mood this morning," says Angel, not looking up from her mobile, "when I left him to shower."

My head whips up at her words. "Shower?" I repeat without thinking.

"Yeah, it's that thing you do to stay clean," snaps Angel.

"Why you always gotta be a bitch?" huffs Piper.

"It's just, I thought you two had fallen out. I heard Hulk say something about Ace being pissed at you." I'm lying, but I need more information without it looking obvious that I'm upset.

Angel gives me a pitying, condescending look. "Oh honey," she sighs, "are you still hung up on him?"

NICOLA JANE

I feel Queenie's and my mum's eyes burning into me. "Don't be stupid, Angel, he's a friend."

"So, then you'll know that he and I are as solid as ever. He spent the night inside me, so I guess it means I'm forgiven." She scrapes the chair back as she stands, a smug look on her face. I bite the inside of my cheek to keep from wailing like a heartbroken child. Piper gently squeezes my leg under the table, and I give her a weak smile. Why wasn't I prepared for this? It's Ace—of course, he was never going to commit to me when he's spent his entire life avoiding relationships.

"Mae, help me choose an outfit for the weekend. If the club gets off lockdown, we need a night out." I let Piper take my hand and lead me from the kitchen. As we pass Ace's office, the door opens. Piper continues to pull me, and I keep my eyes on the ground so I don't embarrass myself, as my tears are balancing on my lashes.

"Mae, I need a word." His voice is low and gravelly. There is no way I can hear the words coming from his mouth, or worse still, have him lie to my face.

ACE

"Actually, Pres, Mae isn't feeling too well. I'm just taking her to lie down," says Piper.

"It's important, Mae. Just a minute of your time, please."

I shake my head, still avoiding eye contact. "I need to lie down."

"Do you need me to get the doc?" he asks, concern in his voice. I shake my head again and let Piper lead me away.

Chapter Nine

ACE

I don't understand women. I never have. Mae is avoiding me. Whenever I go to her room, Piper is there. She's like some damn pit bull, telling me Mae isn't well enough to see me. I feel bad for not turning up last night, but I got a call saying Lorenzo had been spotted, so I had to go and check it out. It proved pointless. The shack he'd been seen at was empty, with no sign of anyone ever being there.

This only serves to remind just how complicated women can be. If she's upset, she just needs to tell me. I hate to be ignored.

Scar pops his head into the office as I'm rolling a pen back and forth across the desk. "You okay, Pres?"

"Just pissed that we didn't get him. I want this to be over with."

"We all do, brother. We'll get him. Everything else okay?"

I frown at him. "What are you asking me, Scar?"

He steps into the office, closing the door behind him. "I came down to get a drink last night. Couldn't sleep and thought a glass of something strong might knock me out."

My heart rate picks up, but I force my expression to remain neutral. "So?"

"I just wanted to say, I don't blame you. She's a beautiful girl, and I'm not judging. Glad I didn't take her out, though," he says, adding a smile.

"Get to the point, Scar," I growl, unsure of how much he knows. Anyone could have been on their knees behind that bar.

"Well, Mae is hot and loads of the guys wanna—"

I stand abruptly. "Don't fucking finish that sentence unless you want me to remove your tongue."

NICOLA JANE

He holds up his hands, a small smile playing on his lips. "Hey, I'm not treading on your toes, Pres. I just wanted to say, I'm happy for you both."

I take a breath and lower back into my seat. Scar sits across from me. "You don't think it's weird?" I eventually ask.

He shakes his head. "No, why would I?"

"Well, because it's Mae. I've known her a long time."

"She's an adult, and so are you. Mae's a great girl and she knows what she wants. You can't pass up someone like her. She knows this life, and you don't get that often."

"I don't know how everyone else will take it," I mutter.

"Fuck everyone else, boss. Trust me when I say, if you've found the one, then you hold on to her. No one's opinion matters."

I'm not sure Queenie or Bernie would agree with that, and at the thought of the two important women in this club, my heart squeezes. I don't want to hurt anyone, especially not them, as they've seen me through some tough times in this club. "Actually, Scar, do me a favour. Come with me and see if the pit bull, a.k.a. Piper, will allow you

ACE

into Mae's room." Scar shrugs, clueless to what I mean, but he follows me anyway.

I stand to the side and watch as he knocks on the bedroom door. Piper answers it. "Hey, Scar."

"Hey, baby, I came to see if Mae's okay. Pres said she was ill."

"Come in," she says, opening the door wider.

"I knew it," I growl, stepping forward.

Piper glares at Scar. "You traitor," she hisses.

"Sorry, babe, he's the President," says Scar, like that's the only explanation he needs to give. I step into the doorway, pissed that I've been refused by Mae.

"You can't just barge in like this," snaps Piper, and I glare down at her.

"This is my fucking club," I snarl. "Get out of here."

She hesitates, glancing at Mae. Any other day, I'd be proud that Piper was protecting her friend, but not today. Today, I need her out of our space, so I can talk to Mae. "It's fine, Piper. I'll be fine."

Piper holds my stare as she leaves the room. It's brave—not many people would stare me down, but I guess she's pissed with me too. It'd be nice to know why exactly. It occurs to me that Piper may be against us, and she might have talked Mae out of trying any sort of romantic relationship with me. That cuts me deep, the thought that Mae might have changed her mind.

"So," I sigh, placing my hands on my hips and staring down at Mae, who's sitting on her bed with her legs curled under her, "you gonna explain what's going on?"

"Nothing," she huffs, and I'm reminded that she's younger than me. I hate the reminder.

"This shit is exactly why I don't date!" I growl.

"We're dating?" she asks, almost looking surprised. "Cos I don't remember going on any date with you, Ace."

"So, you want a date, is that what's wrong?"

"No, I don't want a date. God, I'm such an idiot."

"You're making no sense, Mae, and I don't know why you're mad at me. Just tell me straight cos I can't deal with this bullshit."

"It's fine, yah know, if you're not invested. I get it. I'm young, you're," she pauses and then shrugs, "old."

ACE

"Ouch, get straight to it." I wince and get ready for the blow I know she's about to give me.

"I shouldn't have come on so strong. It's embarrassing and very unlike me. We can't exactly spend the rest of our lives sneaking around. You know Queenie and my mother will sniff out the lie soon and then all hell will break loose. I get that it's too much. We should never have started it."

"You regret it?" I ask.

She thinks for a minute before giving a small nod. I start to back out of the room. She wanted this, and now she's changed her damn mind. I should be relieved. At least if I walk out of here right now, the problem goes away and I won't have to think about how we'll tell people about us. "Right, well, your call. Gotcha, loud and clear, Mae." I pull open the door and take a look back at her. "Sorry if I got it twisted."

Mae remains silent, watching me from her position on the bed. The fact she doesn't bother to correct me or tell me what changed her mind, confirms that we really were a mistake. One that I won't be repeating.

MAE

I take in a painful breath, hurt piercing my heart. How did I get it so wrong? I just assumed, with all the little comments he made, that he wanted more from me, that he wanted to see where we could go. I know he never said we were exclusive, and I'm stupid for thinking we were. I bury my face in my hands, feeling like a moron. Piper comes in without knocking, and when she sees me, she instantly rushes to wrap me in her arms. I burst into tears, unable to keep the pain inside any longer. "I feel like such a fool," I wail.

"Seriously, this is not your fault. You like him, of course, you're gonna throw yourself in one hundred percent. I mean, look at him. Add in that he's the President and phew," Piper wafts her face, "H.O.T!"

I smile through my tears. "I brushed him off. I kept it light and shrugged it off like it was no big deal. I didn't tell him I knew about Angel. I didn't want to sound needy."

Piper strokes my hair. "He looked pissed when he came downstairs. He slammed his office door and the whole main room went silent. It was intense."

ACE

"He can't have his cake and eat it too. I'm not the kind of girl to share. Maybe I should have made it perfectly clear before we did anything together."

"I think we need a night out," suggests Piper with a mischievous smile.

"On lockdown, remember?"

"Lockdown, shmock-down," she says, waving her hand. "We'll get out of here somehow."

"Yah know what, for once, I'm listening to your stupid plan. It'll get us into trouble, but I need a little danger in my life to forget about mister tall, dark, and handsome."

Piper grins excitedly. "Then let's pamper ourselves all day. Get dressed to kill. Have a few drinks downstairs and then sneak out to a nightclub."

My heart hammers in my chest. If we get caught, we'll be in so much trouble, but I need to feel alive instead of this painful regret. I nod, and Piper squeals happily.

We do exactly what Piper suggested. We spend the day in my room applying face masks, relaxing, listening to music, and then eventually choosing killer outfits for tonight. I settle on black skinny jeans that show off my curves, according to Pip, and lord knows I need to feel sexy tonight. I add a red, low-cut top that goes well with my dark hair and tanned skin. After Piper gives me a smokey eye makeup tutorial, I'm feeling confident and beautiful.

As I look in the mirror to paint my lips red, Piper comes back into my room looking just as hot in a tight-fitted pair of jeans and a top that barely passes as clothing and could actually be mistaken for underwear. I raise my eyebrows. "Damn, Hulk might bust a blood vessel when he sees you dressed like that."

Piper smiles. "Good. Let him know what he's missing."

I slip into my heels, and we head downstairs. As we enter the main room, a few of the guys turn to look. "You girls know we're on lockdown, don't yah?" asks Bear.

"Nothing wrong with feeling pretty, Pops. We wanna dress good and feel good," Piper says.

"Okay, just as long as you stay in the clubhouse."

"Got it," Piper shouts over her shoulder, saluting.

ACE

Lucy is sitting at the bar, looking annoyed. She stares us both up and down and whistles low. "Damn, you ladies are looking hot."

"We're dressing to kill. Mainly your brother," says Piper, glancing around the bar until she finds her target. Hulk is staring straight at her, his eyes burning into her bare flesh.

"Well, he looks mighty pissed right now," points out Lucy. She then turns her attention to me. "And who are you impressing tonight, Miss Mae?"

I shrug my shoulders. "Just coming along for the ride."

"Pity we're on lockdown because I think you'd find yourself a man tonight dressed like that." I smile. If only she knew that the only man I want, is her father. The thought brings on that aching feeling again, so I order us each a drink to take the edge off.

We take a seat, ignoring Hulk's burning glares from across the room. I'm not sure why he won't just admit that he likes Piper way more than he lets on. He has serious commitment issues, but it's written all over his face that he wants her. Maybe he's just like his father, wanting the best of both worlds.

NICOLA JANE

"Tag's driving me insane." Lucy sighs. "How come I have to stay here on lockdown, and he gets to go out?"

"Go out where?" I ask.

"To a fight. I hate it when he fights, but he says he can't give it up. He loves it too much, and without it, he can't cope. Thinks he'll go crazy and start being all aggressive. I mean, what the fuck?"

"Well, maybe it helps tame his inner aggressive beast?" Piper shrugs. "He deals with a lot of violence."

"He's the one who's most in danger yet he gets to leave the club. It makes no sense."

"He's Mafia, Luce. He's protected," I say.

"Well, he wasn't protected the last time his father tried to have him killed." She makes a good point, and I decide to close my mouth. She's clearly pissed-off at the moment. She finishes her drink and says, "Anyway, I'm going to bed to sleep off this mood. I love you both. Enjoy the rest of your night, if that's even possible when you're stuck here." She kisses us both on the cheek and then leaves.

"I hope Tag has a lead. It'd be nice to be off lockdown," says Piper. Lucy is new to this life, and it's quite possible that Tag is following up a lead and the fight is a cover-up so Lucy doesn't worry. Glancing around the room, I notice there are a lot of bikers not here, so it's a possibility.

We grab a bottle of wine and sit by the window. I know the moment Ace comes out of his office because my skin prickles like it does whenever he's nearby. My breathing quickens and I try to calm myself. Piper confirms that he's around by whispering and nudging me. I drink the rest of my wine and force myself to stare at Piper so I don't look for him.

"Oh my god," hisses Piper.

"What?" I ask desperately. She looks so annoyed.

"Nothing, don't look," she orders, but the expression on her face causes me to scan the room until I see what she's warning me from. Angel is walking behind him, fastening her shirt up. It's clear from their flustered faces and ruffled hair what's been going on in that office. "Oh Mae," mumbles Piper sympathetically, "try not to get upset."

I square my shoulders and give her an unconvincing smile. "It's fine. We aren't together, remember."

"I know but—" I hold up my hand so she doesn't finish her sentence. I don't need to cry again.

"Honestly, Piper, it's fine. That's what I call a lucky escape."

I watch as they approach the bar, laughing together. Angel takes every opportunity to lean into him as he orders her a drink. Once they each have one, Ace turns and scans the room. Our eyes meet, and for a second, he looks guilty, but it soon passes. He pushes off the bar and heads my way. "Don't leave this club," he orders.

"We're not going to. We're looking for a good time here tonight, Pres," Piper tells him. She adds a wink to get her point across, and Ace turns to me.

"Anyone in particular, Mae? I can put a good word in for you."

"She doesn't need any words when she looks this fucking hot," says Piper, smiling wide. "Pity you blew it, Pres." I glare at her. The last thing I want is for her to antagonise him.

"Piper, your mouth keeps running off at me, and so far, I've let it slide, but if you continue, I might have to remind you who the fuck I am," growls Ace, glaring down at her.

I stand, scraping back my chair and bringing Ace's attention to me. His eyes fall to my breasts. This top pushes them up, so it's hard not to notice them. "Sorry, Pres, she's had a drink. I'll get her some air." I take Piper by the arm, all the while feeling Ace's eyes on me. I walk a little more sexier, making sure my arse sways. "You really have to stop pissing him off, Piper. There are other ways to get to Ace."

"Well, he pisses me off too." She pouts, and I smile.

"Let's get Scar inside and make a run for it. Scar!" I yell, and he steps from his guard box by the gate.

"What's up?"

"Can you run inside and get me a glass of water? This one's had too many wines," I say.

He laughs. "Yeah, no problem. You want a bucket too, so I don't have to wash away the puke?"

I also laugh and then nod. "That'd be fantastic. Thanks, Scar."

NICOLA JANE

We wait until he heads inside and then make a run for the gate, pushing the release button. The second there's enough space for us to get through, we squeeze past. It automatically closes after one minute, and there's no one hanging around to slip in. We take off our heels and run to the end of the road, waving like crazy until a cab pulls over. Once we're safe in the cab, we relax, giggling and panting for breath.

Chapter Ten

ACE

"Why the fuck would I know where there's a bucket?" I snap. Scar has been rustling around behind the bar for the last five minutes. "Why do you want a bucket anyway?"

"Piper is sick, too much wine."

"Jesus, she better not puke near my bike," I groan. "Go check the kitchen."

"I did. Bernie keeps that place spotless, and I can't find anything."

"Piper didn't look too bad when she walked outside," says Angel, running her hand across my chest. She hasn't stopped touching me since we left my office. I sigh as the thought of us fucking just hours ago passes through my mind, and I wince. Being mad about Mae led to me making a stupid mistake with Angel . . . again. "You sure they weren't playing you, Scar?" she adds.

"What do you mean?" I ask.

"Well, they were dressed to kill. Are they breaking out?"

Before she's finished her sentence, Scar and I are rushing for the door. I rip it open and run into the car park. "Mae! Piper!" No answer. I do a three-sixty and see no sign of them.

"FUCK!" yells Scar, realising he's been had.

"Get on the phone to Anton. I want them found. Then get out of my sight, you fuckwit."

"On it, Pres," says Scar, pulling out his mobile and looking sheepish.

I head back inside. Hulk shakes his head with disappointment. "Scar should have known better. Piper is the master at escaping."

"I'm gonna kill 'em." I'm so pissed, I storm straight past Angel and slam my office door for the second time today. Pulling out my phone, I call Mae. It rings out and then her answer message clicks in. "What the fuck are you playing

ACE

at, Mae? Since when do you behave like a spoilt little brat? Get yourselves back to this club right now or I'm coming to find you and trust me when I say, you don't want that."

I disconnect and then instantly call back. On the fourth try, she answers. There's music pumping loudly, and she yells to be heard. "What?"

"Where are you?" The music gets quieter, and I realise she's stepping out. "Mae, I swear to god, get back here right now. I don't know what the hell you were thinking. Do you know the danger you put yourself in, not to mention Piper? You're supposed to be the sensible one, and now, I have to send men to come and find you!"

"Then don't send anyone. I can make my own way back when I'm done here."

"You're my responsibility, and we're in lockdown for a damn good reason."

"Stop pretending like you give a fuck!"

"Mae, this isn't like you, you don't do shit like this."

"I've met a man." She giggles, and my body tenses. "He's hot. And not old." My fist curls. She's trying to get a rise. "I saw you leave the office with Angel. You fucked her?"

125

NICOLA JANE

It's a question, and I don't want to lie, but if I tell her the truth, I'll push her into the arms of another man, and she could be in danger right now.

"Tell me where you are, Mae. I'll come and talk to you. Let's straighten everything out."

"No, we've done talking. Just be honest, did you fuck her?"

"What does it matter? You said we weren't a thing."

"So, you did. That's great, it's fine. She's really pretty, just your type . . . if you like thin and pouty. She'll make you happy." Mae's rushing the words out, and I detect the hurt in her voice. "It's better that I see your true colours now. I knew you couldn't be faithful, I'd heard all the stories, but I just thought . . ." She trails off and sighs heavily. "Never mind. I'm drunk. I have to go, erm, I don't remember his name, but he's coming this way, so I really have to go. We'll be back later, don't worry about us." The line goes dead, and I'm even more mad now than when they first disappeared.

"Pres, we know where they are. You want Anton to go fetch them?" asks Scar through the closed door.

"Get the address and tell him to meet us there." Mae isn't going to know what's hit her.

MAE

I giggle. I'm not usually a giggler, but this guy is hot and brings out the flirty side in me. His eyes are so green, his skin so tanned, and his dark facial hair makes all of the above stand out. I try to recall his name—Alex . . . Antony . . . whatever. Who needs a name? He moves towards me, and butterflies take flight in my stomach. I feel the heat of his body as he steps closer and leans in for a kiss.

"Mae! Mae!" I turn to the frantic voice and spot Piper. She's waving her mobile phone at me, a look of terror on her face. "We have to go!"

"Why?" I glare at her, hoping she'll take the hint and let me get to the good part.

"Because I've just had a call from Lucy. Anton is on his way here."

"Anton wouldn't come here, Pip. He's too important. Why would he come here?"

NICOLA JANE

"Because . . ." She pauses, looking uncomfortable. "Look, trust me on this. He's coming, and we need to go before he gets here."

I sigh and turn back to my handsome new guy. "Sorry, slight complication. I have to go."

"Number?" he asks, cocking his eyebrow and smirking to reveal a dimple. I almost swoon as I pull out my phone, but Piper grabs my wrist and tugs me away.

"Didn't you hear me? He's on his way!" she hisses.

"You're overreacting. What are they gonna—" We're stepping out of the nightclub, but my words freeze when Piper stops walking and I run into the back of her, causing her to stumble forward another step. "What the hell, Piper?"

Looking over her shoulder, I see the reason she's stopped. There's a black car parked out front with Anton and his rather large bodyguard leaning against it and staring at us. Anton folds his arms over his large chest, a smirk playing on his smug face. "Surprise, baby. This brave enough for you?" he asks.

"What are you doing here?" hisses Piper.

ACE

"I'm coming to the rescue. Isn't that what you want?"

"No, you know it isn't," she almost growls, and I make a mental note to quiz her about this odd encounter as soon as we're sober and alone.

"Well, at least it isn't Ace," I whisper into her ear. The rumbling of motorcycles shuts me down, and I groan when Ace and Scar come to a stop behind the truck.

"Now, it gets interesting," says Anton, grinning. We remain glued to the spot while the guys greet each other with a handshake. My heart thumps in my chest, and I suddenly feel sober. When Ace finally turns his face to me, his expression is murderous.

"Told you I was coming," he growls. His tone causes me to shiver. "That's four of us standing right here because of your stupidity. All of us in danger, because of you."

I feel like a scolded schoolgirl. It's the first time he's made me feel younger than him, and our age difference is so obvious. "I told you not to come," I mutter.

"You don't tell me what to do, Mae. You're part of my club, so I had no choice!" He yells so loud that passing partygoers stop and stare. "I expected it from her," he snarls, pointing to Piper, "but you, you disappoint me." His words cut me like a knife. I don't like anyone to be disappointed in me, but especially not Ace. "Take them back in the truck. I can't have her on my bike when I'm this pissed off," Ace says to Anton. "We'll follow the truck." I watch with tears in my eyes as he turns without looking at me again and heads back towards his bike.

"Ouch," mumbles Piper. "Talk about overreacting."

By the time we get back to the clubhouse, I feel so on edge that I have to stop and throw up outside. Piper holds my hair back, but I feel the weight of Ace's and Anton's stares as they pass us and head inside. "Finish that and get in my office," Ace throws over his shoulder.

"Shit. I'm not going into his office. He's as mad as hell," says Piper.

"Why prolong it? It'll be worse if we don't go." I sigh, wiping my mouth with the back of my hand.

"Fuck this shit. We're grown women. If we want to go out, then why shouldn't we?" she asks to no one in particular and squares her shoulders for added effect. I wish I had her fire.

ACE

Inside, I knock on the office door. "Come," he shouts, and we step inside. "Not her, just you." I glance back at Piper, who shrugs and then moves away from me. I glare at her and mouth the word 'traitor'. "Shut the door behind you," he adds. When I hesitate, he laughs coldly. "Don't worry, you're quite safe. Nothing will happen between us like that ever again."

I push the door closed, pretending his words don't cut me. I lean against it, not wanting to be too close to him. He's mad and his words are brutal. I fold my arms over my chest, feeling the need to have a barrier between us.

"Ace, I'm really sorry we went out tonight," I begin, and he leans back in his oversized chair. It gives him a cocky feel and it pisses me off. "But I'm a grown adult. I can leave this clubhouse anytime I want." Ace raises his eyebrow in surprise, almost like he's daring me to continue. "And I can make my own decisions. You aren't my keeper."

Ace suddenly stands, placing his hands on his desk, and leans forwards. His face is red, and I think I've made him angrier. "You're right, Mae, you are an adult. You're free to come and go, and if that's what you want to do, you can leave and make your own decisions. So, pack your shit and get the fuck out of my club." My mouth falls open. His tone is so venomous that it takes me by surprise.

"You want me to leave?"

"If you can't follow my rules, rules that I put in place to keep you safe, to keep us all safe, then it's for the best."

"But I don't want to leave. This is my home."

"Clearly, you felt like a prisoner tonight. I don't want you to feel that way, Mae. I want you to feel safe. Everything I do is for the good of this club. If I put us on lockdown, it's for a reason. Tonight, you acted selfishly, immaturely, and like a jealous wife. This behaviour," he snaps, "is the reason I don't have relationships. I like real women and I hate playing games. It proves what I always thought."

"And what's that?" I ask, biting down on my inner cheek to stop myself from crying in front of him.

"That I'm too old for you. I don't know what I was thinking to even go there. Sleep on what I've said. If you want to leave this club, I won't be stopping you." Ace sits back down and opens his laptop. "You can go now."

ACE

I feel around behind me until I find the door handle. Pulling it open, I stumble back out of the office, my heart and dignity in tatters. Before I leave, I take a deep breath and turn to face him. "I'm glad I saw you for what you really are. I don't deserve to be spoken to like that, and from now on, I'll keep well out of your way. But there is no way I'll ever leave my mum, or this club, because it's my home. I won't go just to make your life easier, so unless you pack my shit up and drag me out of here, I'm staying."

I turn on my heel and leave, slamming his office door hard as I go. I don't bother to find Piper. Instead, I run up to my room, fall onto my bed, and cry into my pillow. Tomorrow, I'll be stronger and I'll treat him like someone I once knew. But for tonight only, I'll allow my heart to hurt.

Chapter Eleven

ACE

I pace the room. I called church and invited Anton and Tag so we could get an update on Tag's father. I still have a club on lockdown, and people are restless.

"There's nothing. No sign, no whispers. He has to be up to something big," says Tag. Anton doesn't seem to agree. Instead, he shakes his head and sighs heavily. He's just as annoyed about this whole thing as me. None of us want to risk our families.

"Maybe he saw what he was up against and scuttled back off to the dark hole he came from?" suggests Scar.

"He won't give up. He wants something, maybe his status back or notoriety for killing the head of the Corallo family," explains Anton. "He won't just disappear. While he's quiet, he's plotting. I just don't know if he's the key behind all this or if it's something bigger, something way bigger than him."

"Well, I can't keep this club on lockdown for much longer. What's the threat level?"

"Take the club off lockdown but keep a high alert. Have men posted on the gates at all times and keep a close eye on the women who are most important," says Anton. I want to tell him that I know how to run my club and that I don't need the Mafia giving me instructions. Instead, I nod and bang the gavel on the table to end the meeting. Anton is not someone I want to make an enemy of, not when he's useful to my club.

Keeping important women safe would be easy if the one I want to protect more than anything was actually talking to me. It's been a week since I pulled Mae into my office and told her to leave. When those words left my mouth, I could have slit my own throat. I was calling her bluff, I guess, but the thought of her calling mine and leaving this club almost killed me. Luckily for me, she hasn't gone anywhere, but she's completely blanking me. If we're in the same room, she avoids any conversation and often turns her back whenever I pass. It's for the best, I know it is, and it makes things easier on me. But the guilt I feel is weighing me down, and if I'm totally honest with myself, I miss her. Because before anything else, we were friends.

I go in search of Dodge. I missed his walk first thing, and he was grumpy with me. That dog is more hormonal than any woman I ever knew. I whistle as I walk through the clubhouse, and I spot him when his head shoots up. He's curled up next to Mae on one of the couches. She's asleep, looking peaceful and beautiful. Dodge jumps down and rushes over to me, which wakes Mae up. She stretches out, and her eyes land on me. "Sorry, I didn't mean to wake you. I was gonna walk him."

"I already did it," she says on a yawn. Of course, she did. Dodge is a traitor and a sucker for Mae and her long walks.

"I hope someone went with you," I say firmly.

"Of course, Scar came."

Scar. Since he learned I stepped away, he always seems to be around her. "You and Scar a thing these days?" I ask, trying to sound casual, but Mae doesn't answer. Instead, she stands and heads for the stairs. I don't think about it, but I snatch her wrist up in my hand, shocking us both. I instantly release her, both of us staring at her arm. "Well, are you?"

"Why do you care?"

"Cos I wanna know if you're fucking your way around this club?" I snap. I know she isn't, and I don't know why I can't just be nice to her. It's like I miss her, pine for her, and the second I see her, I turn into this shithead who insults and upsets her.

"When you start announcing who you're fucking, I'll start telling you who I'm fucking."

"Okay, I'm fucking Angel. Now, your turn," I growl.

"Dickhead," she mumbles and rushes off towards the stairs.

I sigh heavily. "Looks like you're always upsetting that girl lately." It's Bernie. Her arms are crossed over her chest, and she has a stern look on her face, a look that all mothers seem to inherit the minute they give birth.

"We're not getting on so good these days, Bern," I admit.

NICOLA JANE

"Let's walk the dog and we can talk about it," she says firmly, leaving no room for arguments.

We set off towards the park. It's the only rural area we have nearby, and when I say park, I'm being generous. It's an unkempt area where the local kids used to hang out. It has one slide and a beat-up, rusty climbing frame. The grassed area hasn't seen a good cut in a long time, but Dodge loves bounding through it. "I once said to Queenie, many years ago, that I thought you and Mae would marry," announces Bernie unexpectedly.

I inhale sharply. It was the last thing I thought she'd say given the age difference. I'd be more suited to her over her daughter. "I know, I know, it's shocking. Queenie went bat shit, said it would be fucked up, but yah know what, Pres? It didn't seem fucked up. You always had a connection, but since she hit her late teens, that friendship you formed, it seemed tight."

"I'm way too old for Mae, Bern."

"Are you?"

"You don't think I am?"

ACE

Bernie shrugs her shoulders. "I think that if you love someone, age doesn't come into it."

"Whoa, who said anything about love?"

"She's a good girl, Pres. She needs someone good in her life. Every mother wants her daughter to be taken care of."

"I'm not that guy," I mutter.

"You've been that guy, so what happened?"

I glance at her, and she gives me a knowing smile. "I know my daughter, and I know you. I've seen the way you've been around each other lately."

"And you're not mad?"

She shakes her head. "Mae is a grown woman. She makes her own choices, and if she's happy, then I'm happy."

I sigh. "Well, she isn't happy right now."

"Then make her happy." If only it was that easy. Too much has been said and done.

MAE

I stare at my mum in disbelief. We were having dinner together, and she'd promised me steak and locked off the kitchen to everyone in the clubhouse for the next hour. "You said what?" I almost screech.

She tops up my wine glass. "Don't look so surprised. You know I can't stay out of people's business, especially when it comes to my own daughter."

I bury my face in my hands and groan. "You are so embarrassing."

"I just wanted to see what happened to make you both suddenly stop talking to each other."

"It's none of your business, and you should have asked me."

"Like you'd tell me anything. I can't believe you kept it from me in the first place."

"Oh my god, I'm never leaving my room again." Finding out about the conversation she had with Ace earlier is mortifying. A knock at the door brings a smile to her face. She places the wine bottle in the middle of the table and straightens her apron.

"I love you, baby girl. I just want the best for you," she says, heading for the kitchen door. She unlocks it and pulls it open. Ace steps in looking freshly showered, his

ACE

hair damp and his black T-shirt clinging to his muscles, hanging out over his jeans.

"Oh my god, Mum, tell me you haven't set me up," I cry, standing up.

Ace looks between us, confusion on his face. I'm not sure if I feel better or worse to know he was also in the dark about this. Now, I'll never know if he wanted dinner or if he's planning ways to escape. My mum gives an apologetic wave before darting out the door and pulling it closed. "Ace, I'm so sorry. She's crazy." I pick up the empty plates from the table, deciding to clear them away and give myself a distraction from the awkwardness of this situation.

"What are you doing?" he asks.

I look down at the plates in my hand and to the table that is laid beautifully. Two silver domes sit on the table untouched. "I just thought you'd want to get out of here," I say. "You don't have to make excuses, it's fine."

"Bernie promised me a steak, I want my steak."

I bite my lower lip to hide the smile as I place the plates back on the table. "Yeah, I was kinda looking forward to a steak tonight," I say.

NICOLA JANE

"Then let's eat. I'm famished." Ace lifts the lid on the first silver dome. Two steaks lay resting, cooked to perfection. Under the second lid is a tray of potatoes and vegetables. "Sit, I'll serve." I've missed his bossy tone. "Bernie surprised me today," he begins, and I remain quite as he spoons vegetables onto my plate. "She knew we'd had something between us."

"Well, she didn't hear it from me . . . and did we have something?" I ask. "Can it be classed as something?"

He shrugs. "Sex is something."

"Well, my mother is bat shit, so ignore her."

"She said she always thought we'd get married."

I almost choke on my own saliva. Coughing, I pat my chest. "Told you, bat shit," I croak.

"She said she wanted what was best for you."

"And she thinks that's you? Maybe if I told her everything, about Angel and the way you treated me, she'd soon change her mind."

Ace nods. "Yeah, maybe. It's a shame we never talked. Not properly. I've always been able to open up to you, but I couldn't work out how to talk to you about us."

ACE

"Angel told me about your night together," I suddenly blurt out, and Ace looks confused for a second. "The night you never came up to bed. You said you'd been busy with club business, but she told me you'd been with her for the night." Ace laughs, and I instantly get mad. "I'm glad I amuse you."

"I didn't spend the night with her. I had a tip about someone we were looking for and went to check it out. So, you stopped talking to me because Angel lied."

"Why would she lie?" I ask feebly.

"It's not so shocking, is it? Club whore wants President, sees his attention is on a club princess, and boom, she lies."

"But you always have sex with her, so how the hell was I supposed to know?" I snap. I feel silly now, knowing all of this was caused because I took her word for it.

"I slept with her after we argued. It was a stupid mistake, but I needed to get you out of my system and she's my go-to."

I roll my eyes, the thought making me sick. "Well, I hope she was worth it."

"Worth losing you?" He shakes his head. "I'm mad as hell you took her word over mine. I'm pissed you wouldn't just come and ask me straight."

I use my fork to push the vegetables around my plate. "I was upset."

"And now, I'm upset. How can we ever have a relationship when you listen to girls like Angel instead of just asking me? If you're my woman and I'm your old man, then you should trust me. If you don't have that, then we'll never work."

"I've been around men who cheat my whole life, Ace. I watch these guys cheat all the time with the club girls. It was easy to believe her."

"It's nice to know you have faith in me, Mae. I thought we could have something special. For the first time, I was willing to see where we could go. All this," he says, waving his fork between us, "reminds me of how old you are."

I slam my fork down onto my plate. I'm so tired of him pointing out the age difference. "My age seems to bother you terribly. It never would have worked for that reason." I stand. "I should have trusted you, I got it wrong, but I didn't make that mistake because I'm younger than you. I made it because I don't trust men. That's something I can work on, but I can't change my age and I can't live with second guessing everything I do and say in case you see me for what I am, a twenty-five-year-old woman. I'm not a kid, Ace, not anymore, so stop treating me like one. If you want a mature woman who doesn't ever question you, then go and be with Angel. I want a man who accepts me for who I am, and that includes my age and insecurities." I leave him staring after me. *Fuck him*.

Chapter Twelve

ACE

It's business as usual. Things around the clubhouse are getting back to normal, and we're all starting to relax again. Tag's father may have come back into the United Kingdom, but he hasn't shown his face around here. Tag thinks he's setting up his own organisation somewhere else, away from London.

I take my usual seat at the bar just as the door opens and Anton enters. He approaches me and we shake hands. He always looks so official in his expensive suits around here where we all wear jeans and T-shirts. He glances around. "I was looking for Piper," he says, and I raise a brow.

"What for?"

ACE

He eyes me, clearly not wanting to tell me the reason. "Just business."

"Piper has business with the Mafia?" I query. "Well, now I'm worried, Anton." I spot Bear across the room with a pool cue in his hand, staring intently at the coloured balls on the table, working out his next shot. I whistle, and he looks up. "Bear, come on over here."

"Really, Ace," snaps Anton, "it's not a big deal."

Bear joins us and looks between us, waiting for an explanation. "Anton here has business with Piper," I say, and his stance changes. His shoulders lift slightly and his grip on the pool cue tightens.

"Oh yeah, what sort of business?"

I shrug. "He doesn't want to tell me."

"It's really not a big deal," repeats Anton.

"You said that already," I point out, and he narrows his eyes at me.

Bear whistles, and Hulk looks over. "Seriously, stop doing that. Is she here or not?" growls Anton.

Hulk wanders over. "S'up?"

"Piper has business with the Mafia," explains Bear.

Hulk's stare turns murderous. "Oh yeah, what's that?"

"Jesus Christ," yells Anton. "Someone around here get me the girl."

"You know she's part of my club, Anton," I say, "meaning you can't have business with her that we don't know about."

Relief floods Anton's face when Piper rushes towards us, Mae hot on her heels. "What's going on?"

"Tell me what business you have with the mafia?" Bear demands to know.

"It's not business," she huffs. "Who said it was business?"

We all look to Anton, who shifts uncomfortably. "Can you call off your pit bulls," he asks her, like she's the one in charge.

She reaches past us all and takes Anton by the hand. "Come on." She sighs, pulling him to follow her. We all stare, open-mouthed. Bear growls and goes to follow, but a firm voice stops him in his tracks.

"Don't take another step unless you want to be sleeping on that uncomfortable couch for the next month." We all

ACE

turn to Queenie, who looks pissed. "That girl is handling her own shit, and she doesn't need you boys to wade in there."

"What the hell does that mean?" asks Hulk, infuriated that he's being stopped by Queenie.

"That means, boy, you should have claimed my girl when you had the chance. I told you that you'd regret it. Now, you get to sit back and watch her love story play out with a Mafia boss, and I know that's gotta hurt."

"You mean they're—" begins Bear.

"Hell yeah, and ain't none of you boys gonna intervene or you'll have me to deal with."

I catch the smirk on Mae's face as she saunters past us towards the exit. "Are you meeting a cop, just to top our day off?" asks Bear. I know he's kidding, but I still feel my chest tighten at the thought of Mae with someone else, cop or otherwise.

"I'm going to work. I've had so long off that I bet the office is a mess."

"You want a lift?" I ask, since one of the guys would usually take her.

"No, I'm all good." She leaves the clubhouse without looking back. It's how she's been with me for days now, cold and blunt, and I hate it.

"These women are taking over." Hulk sighs. "Maybe we should make the clubhouse a woman-free zone?"

"Then you pair would be banned, cos the fear in your eyes when Queenie came out here, screamed pussy." I laugh.

"I didn't see you yelling back, Pres," says Bear.

I shrug. "I like Anton. I was just letting him know who was boss."

"Great, so now he thinks Queenie is in charge," says Hulk and I roll my eyes. Most of the time, she actually is. That lady can get crazy, but she's also the one who keeps us calm. She looks after everyone under this roof and makes sure we do each other right. She's a true old lady to the club.

Bear goes back to his game, but Hulk takes a seat. "Things still cold between you and Mae?"

"She's history. I'd like us to go back to being friends, but I can't see that happening for a long time."

"Let's hope she doesn't go off with the Mafia too. Before you know it, they'll both be moving out to Anton's huge place."

I ponder this for the rest of the day, and I have to stop myself from driving to Trucker's garage several times, just to check she's there working and not with someone else. It's crazy. I've blown it with her, but I still can't get her out of my head. I crave her sweet taste and her hot body against my own.

I remind myself of the same scenarios over and over to remember why I can't go there. Kids, I don't want any more. I'm too old, but she's still in her prime, of course, she'll want a family someday. Then there's the trust issue she has around men. I spend a lot of time on the road, so will she always accuse me of being with other women? Lucy is another reason. I've only just gotten her back in my life, and if she disapproves, she might decide to go back to her mum's or cut me out of her life. I can't have that happen again.

As if conjuring my girl up, she enters the clubhouse looking tired and stressed. When she sees me, she smiles.

NICOLA JANE

"Pops." She kisses me on my cheek and shifts Abel onto her hip. "Is Mae or Piper around?"

"Well, Mae went to work and Piper is off with Anton. Hey, did you know those two were a thing?"

Lucy scowls, her hatred of Anton clear for everyone to see. When he faked Tag's death last year, she was more than pissed. Since then, she tolerates Anton because of who he is, but she dislikes him. "I need someone to watch Abe."

"Well, I can take him."

She eyes me for a second. I've never watched the baby on my own before, and I'm the first to admit I'm not great with small kids. Give them to me when they're walking and talking and it's not a problem, but a one-year-old is a whole other story. "You sure?"

"How hard can it be? Where are you going anyway?"

"I have some errands to run. I can ask Queenie or Bernie," she suggests, but I take little Abel from her.

"I can take care of my own grandchild, Lucy. We'll be fine, and if I struggle, I'll ask Queenie."

ACE

Lucy reluctantly hands me over a bag. "Well, if you're sure. If he gets cranky, his pushchair's out front. Take him for a walk, he'll sleep in that thing, it's like a magic cure."

I follow her out. "We'll be fine. Take your time."

MAE

I was right, the office was a complete mess when I got here earlier and it's taken me hours to straighten it out. I finally file the last invoice, then look from the office window down into the workshop. Most of the guys have gone for the night, but Trucker is still tinkering away with a motorcycle. I lock up the office and head down the metal steps. Trucker looks up as I approach. "You done for the day, girl?"

Nodding, I hand over the keys. "I'll be in tomorrow. I need to get back to normal and that starts with routine."

"Foxy said you'd been a bit weird lately. She's worried about you."

"I'm all good, Trucker. Got my first real look at heartbreak. It wasn't pretty."

He laughs. "That's not your first heartbreak. I still remember you crying over that little guy who pulled your hair many years ago."

"Oh god, that was Thomas Shunt. I was eight years old!"

"It was heartbreak nonetheless. You announced to the whole club you were gonna marry that kid."

"Huh, maybe I should look him up and see if he's still single."

I leave the garage, deciding to walk back to the clubhouse. It's a warm evening and it's a short walk, but as I cut through the park, I can't help but feel like I'm being watched. Occasionally, I glance around but nothing stands out. There are a few groups of teenagers hanging about, but they're paying no attention to me. I'll let Hulk know just in case, but it's not big enough for me to bother Ace with. I definitely don't want to have to speak with him. I'm proud of myself for the way I've acted around him since our set-up date. I've been civil, but I've kept a coolness that's had Ace watching me from afar with longing in his eyes.

As I get into the clubhouse, I stop in my tracks. Ace is pacing up and down with a screaming Abel in his arms. He looks stressed, and Dodge is following every step while whimpering. I consider marching past him, but Abel looks distressed and it wouldn't be kind on him. "You okay?" I ask, dumping my bag on the couch.

"Not really. Bernie and Queenie won't help me."

I smirk, knowing full well they're both backing me and completely blaming Ace for my broken heart. "Oh sweetie," I croon, taking Abel from him and sitting him on my hip, "Did that nasty Ace upset you?"

"Hey, can we not do that? I'm his Gramps."

"Gramps?" I repeat.

"Yeah, sounds less old than Grandad."

I shake my head and slowly walk around with Abel. His cries slow down and, eventually, he rests his head against my shoulder. "Have you taken him for a walk? He likes to go out in his pushchair."

"Oh crap, Lucy told me that. I forgot."

"Well, let's try it."

We head out, and I fasten Abel in and lay his cuddle toy next to him. He snuggles it and rests his head back like he's tired. We head for the park, and Ace follows with Dodge by his side. We remain silent for the first few minutes. Things feel awkward, and it makes me sad. We are so far past friends now that it's too hard to go back there. After all, I've seen him naked. "We look like the perfect family," he says with a smirk.

"If only people knew," I mutter, rolling my eyes.

"If we were together, would that make you Abel's step-grandma?"

"We're not together," I say sharply. I need us to change the subject, so I go for the obvious. "How's things with you and Angel?"

"Don't do that, Mae," he groans. "It pisses me off when you try to act like you don't give a shit."

"I don't, I'm being polite."

"Are you seeing anyone?" It crosses my mind to lie, but I can't. He'll know by the blush on my cheeks or the fact that I never leave the clubhouse. I shake my head. "Good."

ACE

"So, you don't want me, but you don't want me to move on?"

Ace growls. "Can we have one conversation that isn't an argument?" We fall silent again. The park is now empty compared to just ten minutes ago. Dodge runs off ahead, sniffing every bin and post he spots. "Do you want kids, Mae?"

"Not really. I mean, I can't have them, so I've never really put any thought into it."

"You can't?" He looks surprised. Over the last few years, Ace and I have spoken a lot, but it's something I've never talked about with him. Our talks have always been about Ace and the struggles he was facing.

"I have cysts, polycystic ovaries they call it. I think with medication or some sort of intervention, I could possibly have kids, but if I'm honest, kids don't really interest me. Does that make me weird?"

Ace shakes his head. "Not at all. I guess it's a common expectation to think all women want kids. I mean, you're good with kids, so I just thought you'd want them some day."

"What about you? Can you see yourself having more kids?"

"I'm too old," he says. "Forty is no age to begin again. Having Hulk and Lucy young was out of my control in some ways. I should have waited, done it all properly with a wedding, but it is what it is, and I'm blessed to have them both in my life again. Besides, now I'm a gramps, it just doesn't seem right." Ace whistles for Dodge. "I'm not sleeping with Angel," he suddenly blurts out, and I glimpse up at him.

"Well, it's your business."

"I know, just wanted you to know that I'm not jumping into bed with someone else after everything that happened between us." I can't deny that the news pleases me. I'd like to think he was just as cut up as me, but I have a feeling it's more to do with how she lied to me. "What she did, lying like that, it pissed me off. I don't want to lead her on anymore, and I can't risk her wrecking future relationships." The pain in my chest twists, and the thought of him having future relationships hurts me. It's too soon for me to think of him like that.

ACE

Dodge hasn't returned, so Ace whistles again. We hear a whimper, and we exchange a concerned look, then rush along the path. As we round the bend, we spot Dodge by the park exit. There's a rope attached to his collar, and he's tied up to the metal gate. "What the fuck?" mutters Ace, crouching down to stroke Dodge, who pulls at the rope. He's used to running free as Ace hardly ever puts him on a leash.

There's nobody around and the park is eerily quiet. I wait patiently as Ace tries to untie the rope, but the knot is pretty tight. We're so busy concentrating on that, I don't hear anything until an arm wraps around my neck and I'm pulled back against a hard body. I let out a surprised squeak, releasing my hold on the stroller. Ace looks over his shoulder and stands, immediately pulling a gun from his ankle strap. He points it at me, and I gulp. Something hard presses against my cheek. "Drop the gun or I'll stick this straight into her skull." The voice behind me is low and gravelly, but I don't recognise it. Ace lowers the gun and places it on the ground. "Now, the rest."

NICOLA JANE

I watch as Ace begins to pull out weapons from hidden holsters around his body. When they're all on the ground, a white van pulls up and two large men dressed in dark clothing get out. One collects up the weapons and places them in a bag.

"Now, I'll tell you exactly what's gonna happen. You're gonna get into the van, any funny business and I'll kill this bitch right in front of you. I'll start by torturing her slowly, so her death will be long, drawn out, and painful, and you'll watch every second of it. Are we clear, Ace?"

Ace nods. I've never seen fear in his eyes before, but it's there now. "What about the baby?" he asks.

"The dog can watch it. I'll get a message to your club."

"I can't leave a baby in the park alone," growls Ace, and the guy laughs. It's low and menacing.

"I think you'll find I'm in charge right now. We're gonna move slowly towards the van."

"Please," begs Ace, "don't leave the kid like this."

"You should be thanking me that I'm leaving the fucker alive. You keep talking, and I'll soon change that."

ACE

Ace pats Dodge. "Stay, guard," he orders. Dodge sits by the stroller proudly.

Ace takes a step towards the van, and the man pushes me to follow, his arm still tight around my neck. Ace gets into the back of the van, and the man inside kicks him to his knees. He winces. "Arms up," says the man, and Ace puts his arms above his head. The man cuffs him to the roof of the van through large steel bolts.

I'm bundled into the back alongside him, and the man who has me also climbs in. He sits on a seat and pulls me onto his lap, holding me securely while another man cuffs my hands behind my back.

In the front of the van, the passenger pulls out a mobile and makes a call. He orders the person on the receiving end to contact The Rebellion MC and tell them the dog and baby are in the park and that further instructions will be sent soon.

Chapter Thirteen

ACE

Mae's eyes burn into me. I try to reassure her with a smile as the van engine roars to life. With the movement, I find it hard to stay upright as I swing back and forth. "Who are you?" I growl.

"You'll soon find out. Be patient."

"You've just signed your death card, you know this, right?"

The guy laughs. "Then I'll make the most of this," he whispers into Mae's ear, running his hand down her front. I yell out angrily, pulling hard on the chains, but I'm unable to get near them, and the guy laughs more. "You don't

ACE

like me touching your girl, Ace?" He rests his hand on her breast, and I stare at it hard, anger pulsing through me.

"Your death will be a slow one. I'll start by taking that hand off with a blunt blade."

"Promises, promises, but I'm not the one tied up."

I calculate that it's at least another half-hour before the van stops and we're hauled out. I'm blindfolded and cuffed, then pushed into another vehicle. This time, it feels like a car. "Mae?" I shout out.

"I'm here," her voice quivers from somewhere nearby.

"We'll be okay. I'll get us out of here."

"Mae?" growls another voice. "Who the fuck is Mae?"

"You got the wrong fucking girl," yells another voice. My mind races. The guy in the van referred to Mae as my girl. He thinks that Mae is Lucy. I don't say anything.

"How the hell was I supposed to know? She was pushing the kid, and she has the same hair."

"The boss is gonna kill us!"

We travel some more, and it feels like hours now that I'm blindfolded, but my guess is it's maybe another twenty miles. When we stop, I'm pulled roughly from the car and marched along. I stumble a few times, feeling loose stones beneath my knees. I count thirty steps and then I hear the clanking of chains. We step into a room and a door is slammed behind us, then my blindfold is pulled roughly from my eyes, and I blink until my sight adjusts to the dimness. There are stone steps before us, heading down into some kind of basement.

The guy to my left gives me a shove, and I begin to walk down until I'm in a dark room. There's a dim light, but it doesn't illuminate much. I'm taken to the middle of the room and new cuffs are placed onto my wrists as the old ones are removed. My hands are fixed above my head to another chain. "Is anyone gonna come and tell me what the fuck is going on?" I snap. I'm answered with a blow to my stomach. "I guess that's a no," I growl. "Where's the girl?"

"She'll be along soon. She's meeting the boss."

I pull hard on the chains, but they're fixed to the ceiling with a large bolt. It's no use, I'm not getting out of these anytime soon. The guy leaves, slamming the door hard and locking it.

ACE

Looking around the damp room, I spot a toilet and a basin in the far corner. Opposite me is a metal-framed bed with a thin mattress thrown on top. It's dirty and stained, but right now, it looks more inviting than standing here with my hands above my head.

A short time later, the door opens again, and I hear Mae cry out. The door slams shut and then there's silence. I wait for a few seconds before I risk it. "Mae," I whisper.

"Ace?" she cries out, and I hear her rush down the steps. She throws herself at me, wrapping her tiny arms around my waist. "Oh my god, I thought they'd killed you."

"I'm okay. Are you?" I ask, desperate to see her face.

She finally looks up at me. "What the hell is going on?"

"I don't know. I think they were looking for Lucy. They thought you were her."

Mae suddenly bursts into tears, burying her face into my chest again, "Oh god, what about Abel? Do you think he was okay?"

"Yeah, the club would have come for him. It was Lucy they wanted, not Abel." I don't want to worry her, but I'm praying silently that the club has found him.

NICOLA JANE

"But why her?"

It's a question I've been asking myself since I got put in the van. If it was Tag they wanted to upset, surely, taking his kid would have had a more desired reaction. Tag would do anything for Abel. And if it was just Lucy they wanted, why? She wouldn't upset anyone.

"Where have you been? Why didn't they bring you here with me?"

"I was taken to a room. A few men came in and looked at me, then it all kicked off. They were yelling at the guy who took me, said he was useless, and then they shot him. Just like that!" She begins to cry again, and I wish I could wrap her in my arms.

"Did they say anything to you? Ask you any questions?" Mae shakes her head. "Okay, you need to climb up and see if this bolt is as tight as it looks," I say. Mae stares up to the bolt that holds my chains. It's a good foot higher than me, and I'm just over six foot tall.

"Climb up how?"

"Up my body. As high as you can get." Mae looks doubtful. I bend my knee slightly so she can put her foot on it,

ACE

then she grips my arms and hauls herself up. "Get your knees on my shoulders," I say. Mae grips the chain and uses it to pull herself onto my shoulders. It confirms what I was thinking—the chain is solid. Mae tugs on the chain and then tries to wiggle the bolt, but it doesn't budge. She tries desperately to unscrew the bolt, but again, with no luck. "You know, if this wasn't such a serious situation, this is a great position for—" Mae looks down at my head between her knees and glares at me.

"Wow, I'm glad that's what's on your mind," she huffs, and I smirk. "Do you think we could concentrate on the urgent situation we've found ourselves in?"

"I'll think of something. Besides, The Rebellion will be all over this. I bet they're already on their way."

MAE

It's been at least two days since we came to this hell. The Rebellion are not all over this, and they have not come to our rescue. With each passing hour, I'm getting more and more doubtful. I'm weak, as the people holding us here haven't brought us any food or water yet. The only time they came in was to take turns beating Ace, and even then, they didn't say what they wanted or why we're here.

I look over to where Ace is still tied to the roof. Resting, his head hangs limp, and his light snores fill the dank room. The clanging of the bolt wakes him, and he looks around until his eyes fall to me. I offer a weak smile to let him know I'm still with him.

The sound of heels clicking on the stone rings out in the room and a woman appears. Her long blonde hair shines, even in this low lighting. She smells fresh and clean. Her lips are painted red, and she's wearing a short, tight, red dress that clings to her curves perfectly. She's carrying a glass of water, and I want to cry with joy. "Oh, I heard you were handsome, but the stories didn't do you justice." She smiles, running a red painted nail down Ace's chest. "I'm Mystique." She smiles, hardly bothering to glance in my direction. She holds the glass to Ace's lips and lets him sip. When a trickle spills down his chin, she wipes it with her thumb and then pops it in her own mouth and sucks it clean. "I'm going to be taking care of you, handsome. How lucky are you?"

"What does that mean?" he asks warily.

"Well, a big strong man like yourself needs special attention." She runs her hand over his broad chest and up his muscled arm. "And the boss gave me special instructions to take care of you."

"I don't understand what the fuck is going on. What does he want from me?"

"I don't get to know the details, baby," she croons. She offers him some more water, he takes it and then nods to where I'm curled up on the bed.

"Mae needs some too."

The woman looks me over. "Oh, I've been told not to give any to her. Sorry."

"But if she doesn't drink soon, she'll die. Just a sip," begs Ace. "Please."

"Give me what I want and then maybe I'll consider it."

"What do you want?"

"I think that's obvious, don't you?" She rubs her hand over Ace's crotch, and he shakes her off.

"Fuck you. What kind of sick bitch wants to fuck a man who's chained up? You get a kick out of it?" he growls.

NICOLA JANE

The woman smirks and then tips the glass of water upside down, spilling it by his feet. "You stupid bitch," he yells, tugging hard on his chains. She moves close, gripping his chin in her hand.

"I'll let you think about it. See you tomorrow, stud." She sways her hips as she walks. "I might even bring food with me."

Ace stares at me, and I see the torture in his eyes. "Wait," he shouts, and she freezes, turning to face him with a satisfied smile on her lips.

"No," I croak. "No, I don't need anything that bad."

"Mae, you'll die."

The woman laughs aloud, throwing her head back. "Seriously, you think I need to force men to have sex with me? Look at me. I can't give her water, they'll make my life hell. They want you to suffer, and watching her is killing you."

"What kind of sick fucks are they?"

"The kind that want The Rebellion to suffer."

The woman leaves, happy that her mindfuck mission is now complete. I stare longingly at the water as it soaks into the stone. I'd tried the basin when I first came. The

ACE

knobs turn, but nothing comes out. Just like the toilet—it doesn't flush, so there's no fresh water.

"She could be our way out of here," says Ace. "Maybe I can use my charm to win her over. If I can just get her to unlock these cuffs, I can overpower her."

"With no water or food inside of you, you're weak. Even if you get past her, we don't know who's outside waiting. They'll kill us both."

"What do you suggest we do then, Mae?" he growls, frustrated at the lack of enthusiasm for his plan. My hope is running out fast. We have no clue where we are or why the hell we're here.

"I don't know, Ace. All I know is we're stuck here, and the chances are they're gonna kill us once they're bored of us."

It's the middle of the night when I'm dragged from my bed and pulled up the steps. I stumble several times, cutting my legs and hands. Ace yells and curses, but they take no notice as I'm pulled out into the fresh, cold night. The stars are bright, and I guess we must be in the countryside somewhere. The stars only shine like this when there are no city lights to dull them.

There's a large home nearby. It's where they first took me when we arrived here. It's the sort of home girls like me dream about, with red bricks and white pillars standing proudly out front. Inside, it's clean. The floors shine, polished and buffed until the twinkling lights from the chandelier can be seen reflecting.

My feet are bare, as I somehow lost my trainers in the struggle when we were first bundled into the van. A well-built man in a suit steps out of a side room and grins at me. "You know, you weren't the girl we wanted, but I'm so glad we found you. I think you'll be so much fun. Go and bathe, and I'll join you shortly." I watch as he disappears into another room. The man who brought me in here pulls me up the winding staircase, and the cream fluffy carpet on each step feels amazing between my toes.

I'm taken into a room with a large bed, big enough to get at least four of Ace in. "Bathroom's through there," grunts the man, pointing to another door. I wait for him to go

ACE

and then rush to the bathroom. I turn the cold tap on full and splash the water into my parched mouth, savouring the cool feeling as it slides down my throat.

There's a bath filled with warm water and bubbles waiting for me. I glance back at the door, finding there's no lock, but the water looks so inviting that I'm desperate to feel it cleanse my skin. I strip off quickly and step into the bath, closing my eyes in pleasure as the warmth envelopes me. There's a line-up of small bottles, each containing a different potion to get me clean, and I don't hesitate to use each one.

Once I feel clean, I settle back and close my eyes. It's hard to relax when I know the man is coming to join me soon. It happened the first night I was brought here, exactly like this, only I was in a different room. I didn't tell Ace. It would have hurt him, and he needs a clear head so he can get us out of here.

I dry and pull on the shirt that's laid out on the bed for me. It's a man's shirt, white with buttons up the front. I fasten each one and then climb into the clean bed. I feel my eyes drifting, and the man isn't here yet, so sleeping for a short while can't hurt.

I don't know how long I sleep, but I'm awoken without warning. My ankles are tugged hard, and I'm pulled down the bed until I'm hanging over the edge. Then I'm turned over onto my stomach and a hand pushes into the middle of my back, crushing me against the mattress. I grip the sheet in my fists and squeeze my eyes shut while the man in the suit takes what he needs. This time, I don't waste any tears. Instead, I think happy thoughts. I think of my mum and our holidays to the sea when I was little. I think of my friends and how amazing each one of them is. And I think of Ace, the only man I have ever really loved.

Chapter Fourteen

ACE

Mae is gone for a few hours at least. When she returns, she's clean and fresh, her hair is damp, and she's wearing a shirt, a mens white shirt, and nothing on her legs. I watch her as she takes a seat on the bed. "Where have you been?"

"We're in the countryside. I noticed the stars were shining brightly. That only happens when the city lights are far away. We drove for almost an hour from London, so where could we be?"

"How the fuck do I know, Mae? We could be anywhere around London. It means nothing, and even if we knew, who the fuck would we tell?" I'm pissed. Why is she clean?

NICOLA JANE

Why is her hair damp? I can smell expensive shampoo, and who gave her the shirt?

"The house is big. It's like a country estate. Do you know anyone who owns a big house in the country?"

"Yeah, Mae, I always hang out with the big wigs and play golf at their country manor in my spare time. Where the fuck have you been, and who's shirt is that?"

"Well, think, Ace! Get us out of here. Come up with something, anything to get us the fuck out of here!" She's getting hysterical, her voice high-pitched and shaky. "I just want to get out of here." She begins to sob and then lays down on the dirty mattress, pulling her knees up to her chest.

"Where did they take you, Mae? Did you talk to anyone?"

She shakes her head. "I didn't see any men hanging about. Outside, there wasn't anyone, but the gates are high. Inside, there was just one man in a suit. He looks important and he was the one who killed the guy that took me. I think he might be the boss."

ACE

"A suit?" I repeat. "So, that rules out a biker gang. Did he have tatts?"

She shakes her head. "I didn't see any."

"How much of him did you see, Mae?" I ask, my voice steady and controlled. She looks away, and it's all the answer I need. "Fuck!" I pull hard on the chains, over and over, yelling and cursing. By the time I've exhausted myself, Mae is sobbing harder into the mattress. The sound of my shallow breathing fills the air along with Mae's quiet sobs. "Okay, Mae, we need a plan."

I wait for her to look at me. "What kind of plan?"

"Does he ever leave you alone?" She nods her head. "You need to see if you can get help. Look for a phone . . . maybe steal his. Get something sharp. If we can dig around the bolt, I can get free." She's nodding, her eyes wide. "Anything you can think of that will help to get us free, Mae."

We talk. Mae can't settle, and she tells me about what it was like for her to grow up in the club around all the bikers and women. She tells me things about the guys that I didn't know. Like Scar, for instance, helps out at a refuge for women who've suffered from domestic violence. That one sticks with me the most. I thought I knew all my men, but Scar plays his cards close to his chest. The fact that Mae knows this information gets my mind working overtime. I know deep down it's because we're locked up in here. I'm hungry and so thirsty that my body shakes uncontrollably. My arms ache, and I've lost feeling in my hands because my circulation has been cut off by the tight chains.

We must drift in and out of sleep. I wake when a hard punch to my stomach sets me coughing until I want to puke. Of course, nothing comes out cos there's nothing in there. One of the men who brought us here grins. "Seems your daughter isn't as keen to have pops home as we thought."

"Lucy?"

"Your club doesn't care either. You'd think someone in this world would miss you. Aren't you supposed to be important?" He lands another blow to my stomach.

"You're a bunch of clowns. They'll never give you what you want. First, you take the wrong girl, and then you leave the one thing that could have gotten you what you want behind."

ACE

"Yeah, well, we ain't no kid killers. We're getting exactly what we want, so don't worry your pretty little head, Mr. President." He glances at Mae's sleeping form. "See that bitch? We know she's important to you, so we're gonna start right there."

They've done some homework and it makes me nervous. "She ain't important, you prick. Did you even bother to look into my club?"

"Club princess, from what I hear." I watch as he pulls out a syringe and pops off the protective cap. "So, later, we have a surprise, and it involves this bitch," he hisses, grabbing Mae's thigh and stabbing the needle into her leg. She wakes instantly, but the guy is already withdrawing it. "She'll need her rest." Mae's eyes drift closed again, and the guy runs his hand over her ass. "I hope I get a go."

"What the fuck have you done to her?" I growl.

"Trust me, Pres, she'll be thankful she was out of it," he sneers, heading for the stairs. "Party tonight. Can't wait to see you there."

I wait for him to leave before shouting Mae's name. She doesn't respond. I keep talking to her, hoping to God she can hear me and that the shit he just shot in her isn't enough to kill her. After an hour, her eyes flutter open. "Mae," I hiss. She tries hard to focus, but it's a struggle. Her head lolls back and forth. "This is important, Mae, listen," I whisper.

Her tired eyes blink a few times and then she focuses on me. "They're coming back. They're gonna hurt you." My voice cracks, and I swallow hard. "Baby, are you listening to me? You've done brilliantly, but I need you to listen. They want to cause me as much pain as possible, and now they've worked out who you are, they'll be coming to do the only thing that will break me. Do you understand what I'm saying, Mae?" A stray tear rolls down her cheek, and that's when I know she gets me. She understands what's coming next. "You have to be brave, Mae, for a bit longer."

"You said that before and we're still here, Ace. No one's coming for us. We're stuck here like their playthings . . ." I shush her, hearing footsteps approach on the gravel outside. A light pours in as the door is opened and the redhead struts in. Her silk robe is hanging open, her black lace underwear clearly on show. Her heels click on the

ACE

stone steps as she makes her way inside, carefully carrying a tray. She places it by my feet and smiles at me seductively. "Hey, gorgeous, you miss me?"

"Mystique, how long have we been here?" I croak.

"You know I can't talk to you about that stuff, handsome." She picks up a glass from the tray and holds it to my lips for me to drink from. The cool water eases the dryness in my throat. "Please give Mae some."

Mystique glances at Mae. It's clear she's weak and severely dehydrated. "I'm not supposed to until later."

"She might die. Just a few sips, I'm begging you."

Mystique gingerly approaches the bed and offers the glass to Mae. Mae sips it desperately, and the water spills down her chin and onto her chest. After a few sips, Mystique takes the glass back to the tray and then picks up a sandwich. She holds it for me to bite. I don't want to take the food, not when I know Mae won't have any, but if I want to get us out of here, I need my strength. Mae watches hungrily as I take each bite.

"I was supposed to come in here and fuck you, but then they said that Mae was the way to get at you." Mystique rubs her hand against my crotch. "It's a shame. I was looking forward to it." The lust doesn't reach her eyes, and I know this is all an act.

"What are they planning instead?"

She smirks. "A fun little party of their own."

Mystique leaves but returns minutes later with a bowl. She places it by Mae's

bed and squeezes out a sponge. "I have to wash you, Mae." Mae remains still, and Mystique begins to open the shirt, running the sponge over her body.

"What do these guys want?" I ask. "I can't give them what they want if I don't know what it is." My pleas are desperate and unlike me. If I was here alone, I'd die before I gave anything up to these motherfuckers, but with Mae here, it changes everything.

"These guys, they have shit to prove. If they can ruin your club, destroy the Mafia, it puts them on the map." It's the first bit of information that Mystique has given me. "Your club is in chaos. Your VP is going around in circles and he's no closer to finding you. The boss has inside information. Don't underestimate him." Her tone

ACE

is rushed and low, and she glances around even though she knows it's only us in the room.

"None of my guys in the club would be in on this," I growl.

"Men, no, but what about the women?" she prompts. She stands and takes the bowl of water. "I'll help you, if you can help me, Ace."

Hope swells in my chest. "I'm listening."

"Promise that if you get out of here, you'll take me too."

"Done," I say without hesitation. "Get me a mobile phone."

"Are you kidding? I'm being watched all the time."

"You're not being watched now, so I don't believe that." She's been here a few times alone.

"I don't have access to anything to communicate with the outside world, especially a mobile phone," she whispers.

"Then get me something sharp. I need to get this bolt loose."

She nods. "I'll try."

NICOLA JANE

The door opens and footsteps descend. Mystique glances at me nervously. "I have to go," she whispers, heading for the stairs as two men come into view.

The first smirks at Mystique coldly. "The boss is not happy with you, whore. You've been too long."

She scowls. "The girl isn't responsive. It took longer to wash her."

The man slaps her hard across the face, and she drops the bowl of water across the stone floor. "I didn't say you could speak," he hisses.

"Pussies," I mutter, bringing their attention to me. Mystique scurries past them and runs up the stairs.

"What did you say?" asks the bigger of the two. He wears a cap, the peak covering his face.

"I said," I growl, "that you're a pussy, hitting on women."

The guy rears his fist back and hits me full in the face. My head snaps back and wetness spreads across my cheek. He shakes his fist, and I smile at him. "You hit like a pussy too."

ACE

"Oh yeah?" he asks furiously. He lands another punch to my stomach, and I cough but remain smiling like a mad man. Smiling always unnerves the aggressor. It makes them doubt themselves.

"Forget him," the other guy points out. "He's trying to distract us from his woman."

"Let's see if you think I fuck like a pussy too." The guy grins, and my smile falters.

The big guy pulls Mae's shirt open, but she stays almost lifeless on the bed, not even flinching, and I'm thankful that whatever they gave her earlier has kept her docile. "Come on, you daft bitch," he growls, slapping Mae hard across the face. I pull on the chains, and the guy smiles menacingly at me. It's the reaction he wanted, but it's out of my control when it comes to her.

I watch, my heart twisting, as he tugs her panties down her legs. "This is gonna be the best fuck you've ever had," he whispers, taking his cock from his pants. I close my eyes, unable to watch. I feel a punch to my gut, and I squeeze them shut tighter.

NICOLA JANE

"If you don't watch, I'm gonna start cutting her," warns the smaller guy.

I hear Mae's sharp intake of breath, and my eyes shoot open. She can feel. She hissed because the guy ran a blade over her arm. The cut isn't deep, but it's enough to sting. "That's better," he says with a smile. "It won't be fun if you don't watch the show."

Mae's eyes stare blankly at the ceiling as the guy fucks her. He isn't gentle, groping at her naked breasts and grunting with each thrust. Bile hits the back of my throat, but I swallow it down. I won't give these fuckers the satisfaction.

It takes him all of a few minutes before he's taking his cock in his hand and with a tight grip, he finishes himself off, his release hitting her stomach. "I'll give her half an hour before I send the next one in." I watch the two guys leave, slamming and locking the door. Turning back to Mae, I see her roll onto her side and tuck her body into a tight ball, her back to me.

"Mae," I whisper, "talk to me." She stays quiet. "I'll make them pay, every last one of them. I swear, I'll cut them into pieces for what they've done to you. Please, Mae, talk to me," I beg.

"Not now, Ace, I just want to sleep," she mumbles.

I press my lips together, knowing I'm losing her. "They're coming back," the words clog my throat and I almost choke, "and I can't stop them."

"It'll be okay, Ace. Get some sleep." My heart shatters, the pain in my chest unbearable. I pull on the chains, and this time, the cuffs dig into my hands but I don't care, I don't feel it. I tug harder. If I could just get my hands free . . .

Mae sits up, wincing uncomfortably, and turns to me, "Stop." It's a firm and clear instruction, so I immediately stop. "You aren't getting free anytime soon, so just stop."

"I've let you down," I mumble. Mae lays back on the bed, but this time, she stays facing me. "When you told me how you felt, I didn't expect it. But over the weeks, I've realised what a fool I've been. I wish I could turn back time."

"What would you change?" she whispers.

Chapter Fifteen

MAE

Ace shakes his head. "I don't know."

"Would you give us a go, if you had the time again?" I don't feel ashamed to put it out there, because if we don't make it out of here, at least I'll know.

"No," he says quietly, and I'm surprised that his simple answer still has the power to hurt my heart. "But not because I don't like you. I do, a lot. But this is the reason I don't let people in. You wouldn't be here if it wasn't for me."

"But I'm here anyway. We aren't even a thing, and I'm still here. You wasted time when we could have been happy and enjoying life together."

ACE

"And you'd hate me even more for putting you at risk."

"I hate you for not giving us a chance, Ace. This bullshit comes with the club. Having you would have made this easier because at least I'd know that you loved me."

"Mae," he mumbles, shaking his head, "you make it sound so easy."

"And you make it sound so complicated."

The door opens again, and Ace lets out a string of curses. I fix my eyes on him. If I have him, I can survive this, I can draw strength from him. "Don't let me be alone, Ace," I mumble, and he stares at me with confusion on his handsome face. "Talk to me, about anything . . . just keep talking."

"I don't know if I can, Mae," he stutters. I see the heartbreak written across his face.

"I'll be okay, I promise."

Rough hands grab my wrists and pin me down on the dirty mattress. This time, a light illuminates my face. "Smile for the camera," hisses a deep voice. I continue to stare at Ace as our eyes locked together taking me to another place.

NICOLA JANE

"Scar will use Nicky for this job," says Ace with a smile. Nicky is Scar's best friend in the form of a sharp blade. He loves knives, they're his favourite weapons of choice, and the fact that he names them amuses everyone in the club.

"Only the best for these pricks." I smile back.

"He'll take his time, with small, shallow cuts, so they bleed out over days."

I nod, the thought bringing me comfort. The rough hands squeeze tighter and I wince. "I want to watch when that happens."

"Front row seats, baby," says Ace. Women are never allowed around club business, so it makes me happy that he'll let me have that. A slap to my face breaks our eye contact for a moment, but it pisses me off and I bring my knee up and catch the guy in front of me in his balls. He shouts and doubles over in pain, and I lash out again, my feet kicking wildly. I catch him in the head, and he grabs my ankles. Pulling himself to stand, he climbs over me on the bed. Using his legs, he keeps mine pinned to the mattress. "You stupid bitch," he growls.

ACE

"Fuck you," I yell and spit in his face. He wipes it away with the back of his hand and hits me across the face again. This time, I taste blood.

"Give her a hit," the guy orders. He releases my wrists, and I lash out, hitting the bastard on top of me hard. I scratch his face, making sure to dig my nails in deep and rake them hard along his cheek and neck. "I love a fighter," he says, smiling. Releasing his erection from his pants, he holds my hands above my head and then lines himself up with my entrance. I feel a sharp scratch in my thigh, then the same sensation of warmth that I felt earlier rushes through my veins and the room goes quiet. My body feels heavy. I manage to turn my head to the side and find Ace's gorgeous blue eyes again. I don't understand why they look so sad, and I try to smile and reassure Ace. *Things will be okay.*

I don't know how much time goes by, but when I open my eyes, the men are gone. The red-haired girl is talking to Ace, their voices low and secretive. I can't make out what they're saying because they sound so far away.

"Mae," the red-haired girl is leaning over me, "drink this." She places a glass to my lips, and I drink the water. "Drink more, you need to hydrate."

I try to sit up, but my body aches. Everything feels tender and stiff, and when I touch my face, it feels swollen. Ace is looking at the bolt above his head. He's standing on a crate with a screwdriver in his hands.

"Take these." The red-haired girl holds two pills in her hand, and I shake my head. I don't know what the hell they keep giving me, but I feel like I've gone ten rounds with Tag in the cage. "It's just painkillers, Mae," she says, pushing them into my hand.

"I think I've done it," says Ace. He's digging around the bolt and the dust from the concrete is falling around him. "It feels loose."

We hear a car engine outside and we all freeze. The girl looks at Ace, her expression frantic and panicked. "Oh shit," she hisses, rushing for the steps. "They'll kill me."

Ace works harder, digging out the bolt. I stand and my legs are shaky, but I can't let these men stop us now that we're a step closer to getting the hell out of here. I step

ACE

up onto the crate. It's the closest I've been to Ace in a long time, but it's also the first time I haven't felt the buzz of electricity between us. I ignore that thought for now and proceed to tug on the chains. He's right, they're loose, but not quite enough to get free. "Hurry," whispers the redhead.

The door opens and she groans in frustration. "Get over here," I say, my tone impatient. The footsteps are heavy as they come down the stairs.

I take the screwdriver from Ace. "What are you doing, Mae?" he asks.

The guy appears around the corner, but I don't give him a chance to take in the scene before him. Instead, I stick the screwdriver into his neck. He grunts and his hand goes to the wound, but I pull it out before he can take it from me and stab him on the shoulder. He looks surprised and shocked, like he doesn't know whether to cover his now bloody wounds or grab hold of me. But while he's working that out, I go for the kill, plunging the weapon into him over and over until he falls to his knees.

NICOLA JANE

I stumble back, dropping the weapon and falling onto my backside. It's then that I notice the blood covering my arms and legs. The dirty white shirt I have on is wet through with the sticky crimson fluid. I'm panting for breath and sobbing all at the same time.

The door opens again, and I want to scream out in anger. The man I stabbed is gurgling and it alerts his friend, who runs down the steps until he sees the guy on his knees, covered in his own blood. His eyes shoot to me. "What the fuck have you done, you little whore?" he yells, marching in my direction. The red-haired girl screams as the man grips my hair and hauls me to my feet.

He pushes me against the wall and moves his strong hands to my throat. "Please," I whisper, trying desperately to remove his grip from my neck. He squeezes tighter and raises me off the ground. My feet bang against the wall behind me, trying to find the grip I need to lift myself. I feel my eyes bulging, and right before I'm about to pass out, I see him.

Ace stalks behind the man so silently that neither of us hear him. The chain holding his cuffs is still linked. He

ACE

hooks it over the man's neck, and in one swift movement, he wraps it around tight. The guy releases his hold on me, and I fall to my knees, gasping urgently to get air into my lungs.

The red-haired girl pulls me to stand. "We have to leave," she urges me.

Ace is standing over the lifeless body of the man, his chest heaving. "I need to find them all," he growls.

Mystique turns to him. "No, we don't have time for that. What if they overpower us and we end up locked in here again, or worse, dead?"

Ace looks at me. "I have to. I promised they'd pay."

"That can wait," I whisper, my voice hoarse from my attack. "We need to go."

Mystique reaches into one of the guys' pockets, checking them all until she pulls out a mobile phone and some car keys. "Bingo," she says with a smile.

She takes Ace by the hand and tugs him towards the steps. I follow, wrapping my arms around myself as I step over the bleeding body of the first man. We race up the stairs and break out into the bright daylight. It's blinding, and I instantly cover my eyes. I feel a hand take mine and lead me along the loose stones, then I'm pushed gently into the back seat of a car. Ace gets into the front, with Mystique in the passenger side. "There's a button on the key ring to open the gate," she explains, leaning over Ace and pressing it. The large gates open and Ace starts the engine, wasting no time in putting it into gear and screeching out towards freedom.

Once we get out onto the road, I begin to breathe again. I was convinced we'd get stopped and killed. I keep glancing behind us, but there's no obvious signs that we're being followed. "Are you both okay?" asks Ace.

I nod, my throat still sore, and I'm exhausted. The trauma of the last few days begins to hit me. I rest my head against the cool window as a tear rolls down my cheek. Mystique reaches back and squeezes my bare knee gently. "We're okay now."

Almost an hour later, we stop at the gates of the Rebellion clubhouse. Relief floods me when Bear steps from the gatehouse to check out the car. Ace sticks his head out

ACE

the window. "Call off the search party, motherfuckers, I'm home."

Bear let's out a whistle to alert the other guys, then he signals for them to come as he opens the gates. Ace parks up and gets out. I watch through the window as word spreads and guys start appearing, clear relief on their faces as they greet their President.

"These guys are big," mutters Mystique nervously.

"They're all amazing." I sigh. "Real gentlemen."

The clubhouse door flies open, banging on the wall behind it, and my mother rushes out, covering her mouth as she sobs. "Is she with you?" she asks, and Ace nods, reaching for the handle of my door. He pulls it open and holds out his hand for me to take. Gripping the door, I pull myself to stand, doing my best to avoid touching Ace. He stares at me for a second, but he doesn't get the chance to ask me what's wrong because my mum envelopes me in her arms and sobs into my neck. We're then wrapped in Queenie's arms, and before long, I feel others join us too. "Is Able okay?" I whisper and my tears turn to happy as mum nods.

NICOLA JANE

I never thought I'd be here again. I watch the women chatting happily, pleased we're all together again. The men went into church over two hours ago. Mystique was introduced to the women by Ace, and he made it clear she'd be sticking around and that she's to be treated like one of us. I'm grateful to her for her help, but I don't like the way she's been flirting with Ace. She's made it obvious she likes him.

"Are you okay, sweetie? You're shaking." Queenie gently squeezes my arm.

I nod, though I actually feel terrible. My body aches and I can't control these shakes. Mystique takes my hand. "I'll walk you upstairs, Ace said I'm in the room next to you." She smiles, and I don't have the energy to argue, so I stand, kissing the women goodnight.

We get to my room, and Mystique follows me inside. "You need a hit."

"A what?" I ask.

ACE

"A hit. They must have given you heroin. You'll need a fix or you'll get worse."

I laugh, hardly believing her words. "I don't need a fix. I'll feel better once I've slept."

Mystique shrugs her shoulders. "Don't say I didn't warn you."

Chapter Sixteen

ACE

It's been a long afternoon, with the men updating me on everything I've missed. Turns out it was Tag's father who began all this. He wanted to take Lucy, but instead, he got us. He didn't make any demands on the club or the Mafia. Tag thinks he's trying to gain respect. A man who can take down The Rebellion single-handed would gain respect from smaller organisations. Lucy is pissed with Tag, blaming him for everything, and she's currently living here while he's back at Anton's. I'll sort that mess out later. Right now, I want to find those bastards.

ACE

I sent some of my guys along with Anton's men to the house where we were taken, but it's empty. The two bodies we left there were gone and the blood cleaned away.

I stroke Dodge's head. He hasn't left my side since he saw me. "They knew the club was falling apart," I say. "Someone on our side told them."

"No way! Like who?" Hulk stands. "And we were not falling apart."

"Mystique seems to think it was a female. She overheard a phone conversation, said the voice sounded feminine."

"So, what do we do with that?" asks Scar.

"We keep everything quiet. Nothing gets spoken about out of this room. If they're not old ladies, they can't be here right now."

"That'll put a lot of the whores out. They'll be pissed."

"Old whores, they stay. If they've been here a year or less, they go."

"And what about the new girl?" asks Bear.

"Mystique helped us get out of there. She stays."

I slam the gavel on the table, calling an end to church. I'm dog tired, and I need to check on Mae. The guys leave, and I flop back into my chair. There's a light knock on the door followed by Mystique stepping into the room. She's wearing tight leather pants and a vest that I recognize as Angel's.

"I need to speak to you," she says, closing the door.

"Go on," I prompt.

She saunters around the large oak table towards me, pulling herself onto it. "Mae needs a hit. They gave her heroin, and she's coming down. If you don't wean her off it slowly, her body will go into shock and it'll be very unpleasant for her." I tried not to think too much about what they'd given her in there, but I knew it was something bad. I nod once. "Also," she pauses, "what's the situation between you two?"

"We're friends . . . good friends," I confirm.

Mystique jumps down from the table, smiling. "Good." I let her leave without questioning that remark. She doesn't stand a chance against Mae.

ACE

It doesn't take me long to get what I need, and within twenty minutes, I'm standing by Mae's bed, watching her scratch at her skin while rocking. Mystique stands next to me, rubbing my arm reassuringly. "I won't take it," growls Mae.

"If you don't, it'll get worse. A small amount to ease it and we'll wean you off it slow. I'm trying to get methadone. It's safer, but it's taking too long," I tell her.

"No," she yells.

Mystique rubs a hand down my back. "Maybe we should come back later. She'll be out of it by then, and we can just do it."

"I wanna stay with her until Doc gets here. I hate seeing her like this. She's been through so much."

Mystique nods sadly. "She's lucky to have so many wonderful people around her. You can't sit in here. You're tired and you've been through a lot too. I'll get her mum to sit with her."

I shake my head. She's my responsibility too, and I owe it to her. "I need to stay."

"How about I get her mum to sit with her while you have a short rest, and if anything happens, I'll come and get you. Just an hour?"

"Stop talking like I'm not in the room. You can go," mutters Mae. "I'm okay."

I sigh. "You look like shit."

"You aren't helping, Ace. Come on." I let Mystique lead me from the room. She takes my hand in hers and walks me to my room. I unlock the door and find it's just how I left it. Dodge jumps onto my bed and curls up. I move my head from side to side to ease the stiffness. Having my arms up for so long has strained the muscles. "Come on, sit," says Mystique. I lower onto the bed, and she kneels behind me. "I used to be a masseuse," she explains, placing her hands on my shoulders. She begins to massage the sore tissue there, and I groan in pleasure. It feels amazing. "You have to stop worrying about everyone else, Ace. Take care of you."

"Easier said than done. This place is my life," I moan, closing my eyes.

"And if you burn out, you'll be no good to them."

ACE

She wraps her arms around my neck. "I just wanted to say thanks for everything, Ace. I really appreciate you helping me and giving me a place to stay."

"How did you end up there?" I ask.

"I was picked up in a biker bar." She sits next to me. "I guess I was looking for a biker to whisk me away," she says, chuckling. "I was chosen for the boss, so I felt special." She snorts. "It sounds so stupid now. Anyway, once I got there, he made it clear I wouldn't be leaving him."

"How long were you there?"

"Not long, maybe a month."

I nod. "Well, you're welcome to stay here for as long as you need."

She stands. "Thanks, and if I can do anything for you, anything at all, I'm happy to." She leans towards me and presses her lips against mine. "Anything." I don't immediately pull back, not wanting to upset her, but I'll need to have a conversation with her and make it clear we're not happening.

Once she's left, I flop back onto my bed and let out a groan. Dodge licks my face, and I stroke behind his ears. "Tell me about it, Dodge. More trouble than they're worth."

MAE

It gets so much worse. My body aches so bad, and I can't stop the shaking. Doc comes and injects me with something that he promises is not the same shit they gave me. It takes the edge off, but not for long. It's two in the morning and I'm lying on top of my bed, pouring with sweat and shaking. My mum reaches out and strokes my arm, but even that hurts, so I turn away. "Can I get you anything?"

"I need Ace," I mumble, rubbing my arms.

"Okay, I'll get him."

She leaves and returns minutes later with Ace rubbing his eyes and yawning. "I need it. Whatever you had earlier, I need it," I tell him.

"I thought Doc gave you something."

"He did, but it hasn't helped," I snap, irritated by his slowness. "Ace, I need it now."

ACE

"Mae, I can't give it to you if Doc gave you something already. You don't want to overdose."

I press my lips together before asking my mum to leave us alone. I wait for her to go and then push myself to sit up. "You know, Doc gave me the morning-after pill. He checked for diseases and he's done a pregnancy test."

"Urgh, Mae," Ace groans, rubbing his tired face. "Don't do this. Don't try and guilt me."

"He said it's too soon and the pregnancy might not show yet. I have to redo a test in a couple more weeks."

"Well, we can deal with that if you are, try not worry."

"Try not to worry . . . are you shitting me? You saw what they did to me," I yell. "And now, you won't help me. I can't sleep, I can't eat. I need it!"

"Mae, you don't need that shit. Doc will help you get off it, just give it time to work."

I reach out and take his hand, but it hangs limp in mine. "Please, Ace, I'll do anything," I beg. "Whatever you need, you can have." It takes him a second to realise what I'm offering, and when he does, he pushes my hand away in disgust.

"Jeez, Mae, really?"

"I need it, Ace," I sob, burying my face into my hands.

He grips my upper arms and pulls me to stand, shaking me until I uncover my face. "You don't fucking need it, Mae. Sort your shit out!"

I begin to cry harder. He doesn't understand how much this hurts. "Go back to Mystique," I shout, trying to push him away. "Get out!"

"What are you talking about now?"

"I saw how you were together. You want her."

I fall back onto my bed when he releases me. He's never looked at me like he's looking at me right now, with so much disgust. I force myself to look away.

My mum knocks on the door. "Everything okay?"

"No, Mum, it's not. I want him to leave," I sob.

Ace opens the door. "No one comes in and no one leaves this room." He hands her my door key. "Lock it from the outside and give the key to Hulk. Only Doc gets a pass."

"No," I scream, rushing to the door, "don't leave me in here." Flashbacks of the dark cellar fill my head and I beat my fists against Ace's back. He kicks the door closed and pulls me into his arms.

"I ain't going nowhere, baby, not until you're better."

Ace goes into my bathroom, and I hear the shower turn on. Then he comes back to get me, lifting me into his arms and carrying me like a child into the bathroom. I bury my face into his chest. "A cool shower will help," he whispers. He steps into the cold jet spray, not bothering to remove any of our clothes. I hiss as the water soaks my pyjamas, saturating them through.

Once Ace is satisfied that I'm wet enough, he steps out and sits me on the side unit. "Get out of the clothes, and I'll find you something dry to wear." When he returns, he freezes at the sight of me. I hear his sharp intake of breath as I stare at myself in the mirror. I'm littered in bruises, bite marks, and small cuts. My face is swollen and both my eyes are black. "Get dressed or you'll catch a cold," he mutters, placing my pyjamas on the side and leaving.

I dress and go into my room, where I find Ace sitting by the window, staring intently out into the night. I silently climb into the bed. He looks deep in thought, and I don't want to interrupt him.

I lay awake, shivering and shaking. Eventually, Ace sighs and makes his way over to me. Lifting the sheets, he climbs in behind me and wraps himself around me. I don't say anything, but I'm grateful for his closeness. The nightmares that await me may not come if I'm in his arms.

Sometime later, I wake screaming. It's not a scared scream—it's a blood-curdling, horrified scream as I fight my way out of the sheets that are wrapped around my legs and restricting me. Ace is by my side in seconds, hushing me and stroking my sweat-soaked head.

"I was just in the toilet," he whispers. "You're okay." I grip him to me, wrapping my arms around his neck and breathing in his scent. His musky aftershave calms me instantly. "It's okay, baby," he soothes.

The rest of the night goes the same way. I sleep for maybe half an hour and wake screaming with Ace whispering words of comfort into my ear. When the sun rises, I'm exhausted, but I don't go back to sleep. That's where the nightmares await. Instead, I pull a sheet around myself and take a seat by the window. I used to love watching the busy London streets. Our clubhouse is set a little off the main streets, but factories nearby create a lot of passing traffic and workers heading that way. Today, as I look out, I want to scream at them. Why are they carrying on with everyday life when my world has fallen apart? How can things be so normal yet so messed up? I'm jealous that they can go to work and be free of the images that litter my thoughts.

"You're awake," yawns Ace, stretching. "How are you feeling?"

"Tired, dirty, pissed-off, angry... how do you think I'm feeling?" I'm snappy and irritated. I don't mean to take it out on Ace, but it's a stupid question and I have so many feelings, I'm not sure which is the correct answer.

"I meant are you still craving?"

"Yes, of course, I am. It doesn't just stop."

Ace sits up, swinging his legs over the edge of the bed and rubbing his face. He looks tired despite having just woke up. "What happened was shit Mae, and I was right there with you, but don't take it out on me. I'm here to support you."

"Nobody asked you to be here."

"You want me to go?" I nod and turn back to the window. He won't leave me alone, he's too stubborn. He pulls out his mobile as I watch his reflection in the window. "Hey, sorry, man, I know it's early. Can you come and let me out?"

I whip my head around. "You're going?"

"Thanks, man, I owe you." He disconnects the call and stands. "You want me to go, you just said."

"Fine, leave me alone. I knew you didn't care."

"Christ, woman, say what you mean. I'm not a damn mind reader."

The sound of the key in the door gets my heart racing. I remember how badly I need a hit, so I stand, waiting for Hulk to open it. "Good morning," says Hulk in a cheery voice. I make a dash for the door, but Ace had already guessed my move and he hooks his arm around my waist and pulls me to him.

"Not so fast, baby," he whispers.

ACE

"I need some air," I growl, trying to push his arm away.

"Then I'll open the window."

"I want to walk."

"Not yet. You need to stop shaking first. Get this shit out your system and then you can go for a walk wherever and whenever you like."

"Ace, please," I begin to cry again. I've never cried so many tears in such a short space of time.

"Pres, we could walk her around together," offers Hulk sympathetically.

"She doesn't want a walk, she wants to get her hands on that damn needle."

"I don't," I cry, "I promise."

Ace wipes my tears with his thumbs. "Fine, just around the clubhouse. Five minutes and then back in here. Doc will be here soon."

Chapter Seventeen

ACE

We walk Mae around like a damn dog. She can't stop shaking, and she's still scratching at her arms like her skin is crawling with insects.

Hulk takes her back to her room. She's tired, but I doubt she'll sleep. I tell her I have work to catch up on, and though I have no intentions of working, I can't sit in that room watching her claw at her skin. I don't know how to make her better, and I feel helpless, more helpless than when I was hanging from the ceiling while she was being raped. Then, I had no choice, but now, I'm walking free and I still can't help her. I want to take away her nightmares because God knows she's getting them bad. I sat every hour throughout the night with her as she screamed and lashed out.

Hulk enters the office and takes a seat. "Shit, man, she's a mess."

I sigh. "Yep."

"Do I dare ask what the fuck they did?"

"I'm sure you can imagine. They did it to break me. Why the fuck would they do that? They didn't want anything from us apart from breaking the club apart. They could have killed us."

"They fucked up. They weren't after you really. It was Lucy they needed."

"I need to sort out that shit too. How's Tag?"

"Like a bear with a sore head, yelling at everyone, fighting, drinking. He wants her back."

"Of course, he does. Lucy's just upset, but she'll come around. She loves Tag."

"What about you and Mae, is there anything going on there?" I shake my head, and my heart aches in my chest. How can there ever be anything now? It was my fault she ended up in that place. "Do you want there to be?" I shrug, and Hulk smiles. "Well, it's not a no, so surely there's hope there."

"We've been through too much. She's been through too much. How can she want to be with me after what's happened? Just being connected with me put her in that position."

"It's our life, Pres, and Mae loves this life. It's all she's ever known. If she wasn't with you, she'd be claimed by another biker and be happy about it. It's the life she wants."

"That doesn't make it okay, and it doesn't make me feel any better. If she knows what's good for her, she'll get the fuck out of this life and move far away from it. She deserves a happy ever after that I can't give her," I say.

"You sure about it?"

"I don't do happy ever after. She needs a house and a man who's got a nine-to-five job. She needs two kids and a puppy. She needs someone her own age."

Hulk laughs. "Sounds like you've got it all worked out." He stands and walks to the door. "Just one problem with your life plan for Mae."

"And what's that?"

"It's not her plan, it's yours. She wants this life, she wants you, and every time you turn her away, hoping she'll go for that other life, you break her heart. Just love her, Pops. It's all she wants."

He leaves, and I sit back in my chair. I know what he's saying is true. Mae loves this life, although I'm not sure she still feels like that after everything. I open my drawer and look at the expensive bottle of malt I keep in there. After running my finger over the golden label, I grip the bottle neck. It's not even ten in the morning and I'm reaching for the bottle. I pull my hand away and slam the drawer, annoyed with myself for even thinking about it when she's up there going through hell.

There's a light knock on the door and Angel saunters in. "I haven't had a chance to tell you how much I've missed you." I watch her as she moves closer, her hips swaying seductively.

"I thought I said all club girls had to leave the clubhouse."

"I didn't think that meant me." She pouts, touching her chest and twirling the necklace I gave her a few months ago as a birthday gift.

"What makes you so special?" I ask. She perches on the edge of my desk and places her foot on my chair, between my legs.

"You know what makes me special," she purrs, rubbing her toes against my inner thigh.

"Instead of talking, why don't you remind me?"

Angel smiles and stands, lifting her dress over her head in one swift movement. She's an expert in seduction, one of the things that first caught my attention. She rolls her panties down her thighs, taking her time, then she stands before me naked and does a slow turn. "What would you like me to do?"

"You can't do much if I'm fully clothed," I point out, and she grins.

"Let's rectify that right now." Reaching for my belt, she unfastens it and then tugs at my zipper. She rubs my erection through my jeans, and I hiss in appreciation. I need this release, I'm too uptight and on edge.

ACE

I watch as she takes out my cock. She runs her hands up my thighs, raking her nails across my skin, and then she licks the tip of my erection. I let my head fall back and sigh as she sucks me into her mouth. I close my eyes, but instead of pleasure ripping through me, my mind is filled with images of Mae. They're not pretty images, and I sit up suddenly, taking Angel by surprise. "Sorry," I apologise, tucking my flaccid cock back in my pants. "I can't do this right now."

I stand, and Angel begins to dress quickly. "Did I do something?"

"No, it's me. I'm just tired," I explain, waiting until she's fully dressed again before ushering her out the door. I lean back against it, groaning in frustration. Maybe I need someone not connected to this club, an unknown face I can spend one night with and then forget about.

I spend a few hours going over the books for the club, then I send a text message out to some of the guys, including Tag, asking if they'd like to meet for a drink in the clubhouse bar later. I need to get drunk and get laid. I fix a sandwich and head up to Mae's room. Scar is sitting outside on the floor, facing her closed door.

"Everything good?" I ask.

"Yeah, Pres. She was asleep last time I checked. Doc came and gave her something, but she wasn't very nice about it. She's like a different person."

"She's been through a lot. I'll speak to Doc about getting her some counselling."

"The good news is, he said she should start to feel better within the next day or two. He reckons she wasn't exposed to much of the stuff."

"Good. Let me in, I've got her some food."

Scar unlocks the door, and I step inside. Mae is laying naked on top of her sheets. I slam the door quickly before Scar gets a proper look, but the noise wakes Mae and she sits up. "Fuck, Mae, put on some damn clothes," I hiss.

She flops back on the bed and rolls onto her side. "I was hot."

ACE

"Anyone could walk in." I throw a sheet over her. I hate seeing her bruises, they're a reminder of how I didn't protect her.

"I know I disgust you. I disgust myself," she mutters.

"Don't talk shit, Mae," I mutter, placing the tray of food on her bedside table.

"The bruises remind you of what happened."

"Of course, they do, I know how you got them. It doesn't mean I'm disgusted, but it hurts me that you got hurt."

"You won't even look me in the eye," she huffs.

"I got you some food." I sigh. "Try and eat something."

Mae throws the sheet from her body and sits on the edge of the bed. "Look at me, Ace."

I place my hands on my hips uncomfortably and look to the ground. "Just eat."

"Look at me. If you aren't disgusted, then fucking look at me."

I look into Mae's eyes. "There, happy now?"

She grabs my head in her hands and forces me to look at her naked body, "Here," she growls. "Look here." I try to pull away, but she fights me, "Say it. Say you're sick to your stomach. Tell me how you can't even look at me because I remind you of the things they did."

We struggle against each other, her pulling me to look and me tugging to get away. I take her wrists in my hands, and she releases the grip on my head. I keep hold of her wrists and push her against the wall gently. "I'm not disgusted, Mae. I'm not sick to my stomach. I look at you and I want to fuck you. I want to lay you on that bed and make love to you so bad that I disgust myself, because that's the last thing I should be thinking," I confess angrily. "You're gorgeous. No amount of bruises can turn me off your sexy body, but they remind me how I didn't protect you, and *that* is killing me."

I hear her slight intake of breath. "Kiss me," she whispers.

I shake my head. "No, that's the last thing I should do."

"Please, Ace." Tears fill her eyes. "I feel so ashamed and dirty. I want to feel how I did before."

I take her face in my hands. "You have nothing to be ashamed of. You haven't done anything wrong. You aren't dirty. You're amazing and strong... so much stronger than I could ever be."

Mae moves closer, stretching up on her tip-toes. I don't move forward to meet her, but I don't pull away either. Her lips brush gently over mine and still I don't move. This needs to be on her terms. She sweeps her tongue across my bottom lip, and I automatically open for her to deepen the kiss. It's slow and gentle, like she's unsure, but I let her take her time. My heart pounds in my chest as I keep our bodies from touching. I don't need her to know about the bulging erection she's given me.

When she pulls away, she looks shy and bashful. "Thank you."

I smile. "Anytime. Glad to be of service," I joke. "Now, eat something. I'll come back in the morning."

Mae looks alarmed. "You aren't staying?"

I instantly feel guilty. "I have plans. But good news, Doc reckons you'll be feeling more like yourself in the next couple days. I mean, you're looking much better already."

"Plans?" she repeats.

"I can cancel. It was just a catch-up with the guys."

She's already shaking her head. "It's fine. I'll see if Piper is free. I'm not your problem."

"Mae, it's not that. You aren't a problem. I just thought that maybe you were getting sick at the sight of me." Mae wraps the sheet around herself. "Honestly, Ace, it's fine. I'll be fine."

I'm not convinced by her act, but I think it's safer for us both if I stay away from her tonight. Our kiss is burnt into my brain.

MAE

I wasn't going to ask Piper to come, but Ace took it upon himself to invite her on my behalf. I said it just to ease his conscience, but I only really want to be around him. I feel like nobody else understands.

"Things got crazy while you were away." Piper is flicking through a magazine and chatting like nothing's happened. "Tag and Lucy split up, she was so mad at him."

"Why?"

Piper looks up from the magazine. "Because she said it was his fault you went missing."

ACE

"But it wasn't," I say.

"It was Tag's dad behind it. They wanted Lucy. She was so mad that they left Abel in the park like that."

"Shouldn't she be thankful they didn't take him too?"

"I guess so. The trauma sent her crazy. She won't even come up here and see you. She totally feels guilty."

"I don't blame anyone." I sigh. "It happened, it's over. We all need to move on."

"Are you okay?" she asks. "I mean, really okay?"

I shrug my shoulders. "I guess. I keep having nightmares and I don't want to close my eyes. Doc talked about seeing a counsellor. Maybe it'll help."

"You must have been so scared."

"Is it crazy that I'm glad it happened to me and not you or Lucy, or any of the other girls?"

She smiles and takes my hand. "That's because you're so nice, and that's how I know you'll get through it, Mae. You're strong."

"I don't want to talk about me or what happened. Can we pretend we're like we were before? Tell me about Anton."

"Anton?" she asks, looking alarmed. "What about him"?

"Well, you and he are—"

"Are nothing."

"You aren't a thing?"

Piper groans and flops back onto the bed. "Oh, Mae, it's such a big mess."

I smile. "Only you could have a hot Mafia boss on your ass and complain."

"I like him a lot, but something else happened, and he's not going to take it well."

"What happened?"

Piper opens her mouth to answer, but the click of the key in the door interrupts us. Scar pops his head around the door and asks, "Up for another visitor?"

I nod, and he steps back to let Lucy in. She looks at me sheepishly, fiddling with her hair. I stand and smile warmly. "Come here." We hug tightly.

"I'm so sorry," she sobs into my hair, her body shaking.

"Lucy, please don't apologise. None of this was your fault. It wasn't anyone's fault apart from Lorenzo's."

ACE

We hug until I feel her sobs subside. "I'm sorry I haven't been to see you. I felt terrible."

We sit on the bed. "Lucy, I don't blame anyone. I'm glad they took me and not you. I just wish we could've protected Abel more."

"Don't yah think it was weird they left him in the park like that?"

I shrug. "I think somewhere deep down, Tag's dad has a conscience. Abel is his grandson."

"Tag said he probably wants to keep him to run his empire. What the hell did I marry into?" I exchange a snigger with Piper, and Lucy groans. "I know what you're thinking. Yes, I married a Mafia boss, but I didn't think it through properly. Now, I have Abel, so it's not just me I'm thinking about. Will I always have to watch over our shoulders in case he comes for Abel once he's older?"

We don't have the answers for her. We grew up in this life and that was the first time I'd ever been in danger like that. "How's Tag taking the breakup?" I ask.

"Like typical Tag. Calling me constantly, showing up wherever I am . . . he's basically stalking me."

"I wish he'd stalk me." Piper smiles, and Lucy gives a playful scowl.

"Lucy, you and Tag are meant to be. You've punished him enough, now go make it right," I say.

"No, I want to be single like you. We can move in together."

I laugh. "We both live here already. I hate being single. Why would you choose that when you have a gorgeous husband like him?"

"I thought you loved single life? You always seem so happy."

"Looks can be deceiving. The man I want doesn't feel the same."

Lucy looks intrigued. "Is he a biker?"

I nod, and she claps her hands excitedly. "Let me guess," she taps her chin, thinking, "Scar."

I shake my head. Scar is the obvious choice as we get on well and he's more my age. I can't tell Lucy the truth because I don't know how she'd feel about it, but before she can take another guess, Piper rolls her eyes. "It's Ace."

ACE

My mouth falls open, and my eyes burn into Piper's head as she continues to turn the pages on her magazine.

"Piper!" I screech, my face turning crimson with embarrassment.

"Oh," says Lucy, raising her eyebrows.

"What?" asks Piper innocently. "She needs to know."

"Why? It's not like anything's gonna happen between us."

"Oh please, the guy loves you. You'd think the pair of you would just give in already. Life's too short. You've just found that out yourselves."

"I didn't see that coming," admits Lucy, still looking shocked.

"Are you mad at me?"

"Why would I be mad? You've known him a lot longer than I have. He's my dad by blood, but I'm still getting to know the real him. Does he know how you feel?"

Piper smirks. "Just about everyone knows how she feels, including the big man himself."

"And he doesn't feel the same?"

NICOLA JANE

I shake my head. "Sometimes I think he does and then he kind of friend-zones me. Age bothers him."

"He's been single for so long, maybe he's just scared to commit," suggests Piper.

Whatever the reason, I can't imagine we'll ever make it after what he's seen. We shared something so brutal and painful, and now, it's all he can see when he looks my way.

Chapter Eighteen

♥

ACE

It's late, I'm drunk, and the poker game did not go my way. The whiskey bottle I took from behind the bar hangs loose in my hand as I stagger out into the club's car park. I slide down the side of the gate hut until my arse hits the ground.

Bear is out here tonight, but he's patrolling the perimeter. Dodge sits by me, and I stare up at Mae's bedroom. The light is on, but I've had regular updates from Scar, so I know the girls left her an hour or so ago.

"Hey, handsome, what yah doing out here on your own?" Mystique saunters towards me.

NICOLA JANE

"I needed some air after that poker game," I say, swigging from the bottle.

"Mind if I join yah?" I shake my head, and she slides down next to me and plucks the bottle from my hand. "You look sad," she states.

"Don't psychoanalyse me, Mystie. I'm too fucked-up for that."

"I've met many men in my life, Ace, and you're not as fucked-up as you think."

I sigh. "You don't know the shit I've done."

"Maybe sometime you could tell me about it?" She places her hand on my knee, and I eye it suspiciously. "I'd like to get to know you better, Ace."

"There's not much to know." I take the bottle back and drink, trying to think of a way to break the news to her before she hits on me.

"Let me be the judge of that." I feel her eyes on me, so I turn to look at her, taking a second to focus my eyes on her face. "I'm gonna lay my cards on the table."

"Don't do that. Why do women keep doing that to me?" I groan.

ACE

"I want to get to know you properly, Ace, maybe spend some time alone." She leans in and plants a kiss on my lips. I freeze, and she takes that as a green light, locking her lips over mine and thrusting her tongue into my mouth. After a few seconds, I gently push her away.

"Sorry, Mystique, I think you have the wrong impression. I like someone, maybe even love them. I can't get to know you like that. It's not fair to either of you."

"Oh, right. It's just, you said you were single and available."

"I am single, but I'm not available. If I gave you that impression, I'm sorry. My head is fucked with it all."

She smiles, squeezing my hand gently. "Thanks for being upfront, Ace. If it doesn't work out with her, you know where I am."

I return her smile and rest my head back against the shack. I make out Mae's shadow in her window. The curtain suddenly falls back into place, and I realise she's seen me with Mystique. I sigh heavily and then push to my feet. I need to see her.

NICOLA JANE

Making my way upstairs, I bounce from one wall to another, trying desperately not to spill the contents of the bottle. I reach her room, and Scar dangles the key out towards me. "You sure you want to go in there like this?" I nod, resting against the wall. "It's a bad idea, Pres. You'll fuck it up."

"I've done that, over and over," I groan.

He unlocks the door, and I stumble inside. Mae is in her bed, her back to me. "Can I come in?" I slur.

"You're already in," she mutters, not moving to look at me.

"I love you, Mae." I blurt it out before Scar has even closed the door, but, fuck, it feels good to say it out loud.

She sighs. "Sleep it off, Ace."

"No, I really do love you." She ignores me. I begin to undress, falling about and unable to keep my balance.

"I put the message out there that I want to meet up with him face to face," I mutter, and Mae turns to look at me.

"Tag's dad?"

"I'm gonna gut that bastard," I add.

"No," she snaps, "don't meet him."

ACE

"After everything that happened, I have to."

"You don't. Let Anton deal with him. You don't have to be the fucking hero in this story."

"I watched my woman being raped," I growl. "I'll slice him from head to toe and laugh while I do it."

"Don't do it for me. You saw what he did to Tag, his own son. He'll kill you and then I'll have lost you too."

"I'll die with his blood on my hands, and that will make me one happy motherfucker." Mae huffs and pulls the sheet over her, turning away from me. "He has to pay, Mae. I can't close my eyes without picturing them on you." My voice cracks. "It's fucking with my head."

She reaches behind her until she finds my hand. She pulls it, and I lay down, tucking myself around her shaking body. She cries quietly, and for the first time in my adult life, I feel a tear roll down my face. This has broken us both, and I don't know how to make it better.

"I want you to have a house and a puppy. A husband with a good job."

"Like Lucy had with Noah? Acting like the perfect couple in public and then behind closed doors it was a different story? I want an honest man who loves me unconditionally and fiercely."

"Mae, you don't know what you're getting into. You say fiercely, but I lose control. My obsession with you will become unbearable. It's already started. I can't be with anyone but you. I tried and I couldn't."

"I saw you kiss Mystique."

"She kissed me," I say defensively. "I told her I loved someone else. But before that, I tried to be with Angel, but I couldn't. You're in my head all the damn time."

"Then stop fighting it, Ace."

"I'll take you and keep you. Possess you, drive you crazy."

She turns in my arms, her eyes filled with hope. "All I'm asking for, is that you try."

"What if we try and I drive you nuts? I won't let you walk away, Mae."

"I won't walk away. Don't you get it? I love you. I always have."

I release a shaky breath. "I love you too."

She smiles, and it's the first smile I've seen on her gorgeous face in days. "Sleep on it. You're drunk, and I want a sober discussion." I nod, placing a kiss on her nose and snuggling behind her. I feel lighter than I have in months.

MAE

I barely sleep. Mainly because of nightmares and flashbacks, but also because I keep going over our conversation. Smiling, I climb from bed and head for the shower. It's the first morning that I've felt more like my old self. I don't feel sick or weak, and although I am tired, I'm happier than I have been in a while.

Ace is still sleeping, so I dress quietly. He was so drunk that I'm sure he'll suffer a hangover today. Once I'm ready, I creep over to where he sleeps and place a gentle kiss on his cheek. He stirs, stretching his arms out and then groaning when the light hurts his bloodshot eyes. I smile with pity, I hate hangovers. "Shall I ask my mum to bring you her hangover cure?"

He shakes his head, letting out another groan. "No, I can't stomach the thought of raw egg and whatever other shit she mixes in there."

"She loves a potion," I say. "I used to think she was a witch."

I wait patiently while Ace showers. I can't hide the fact that I'm disappointed. I was hoping he'd wake and want to discuss our conversation from last night, but he didn't so much as kiss me on the head as he passed me for the bathroom.

When he returns, he's already dressed in last night's clothes. "I'm gonna go and get changed," he says, rubbing his hair with the towel. "Do you want some breakfast brought up?"

"Actually, I thought we could go downstairs and have breakfast *together*," I suggest, hoping he'll take the hint.

"I'm not all that hungry, Mae. I feel sick as a dog. Speaking of dogs, I need to take Dodge for a walk."

"Well, I could come."

"I don't think you're ready. I'll send Doc up and then ask Mystique to bring you some breakfast."

"Is she staying?" I ask, changing the topic. I'd meant to ask before, but somehow, it slipped my mind. I'm grateful that she helped us get out of there, but I don't trust her like Ace seems to, and I certainly don't like the way she is around him.

"Yeah, I told her she can stay as long as she likes. We owe her, Mae."

"We don't really know her."

"We don't know a lot of people we take in here. We give people a chance, and I like her. She's had a tough life, she deserves a break." I nod, my heart sinking. With no mention of our conversation last night, I'm beginning to think he's forgotten since he was really drunk.

"Well, can I leave the room today? I feel so much better."

"Let Doc take a look, and if he's happy with your progress, then I don't see why not." A small victory at least. I need to get out of this room.

Ace leaves without kissing me or telling me when he'll be back to see me. Doc comes in and does his usual checks. I tell him I feel much better, and he agrees that I'm perhaps over the worst of it. I'm instructed to take it easy for a few more days, but he's happy for me to leave my room. He does another pregnancy test because I keep pestering him to put my mind at rest. It's negative, which again is more good news. He insists we do another in a week's time, even though this test is one of the good ones that tells you how far along you are. I feel confident that I'm in the clear.

It's weird venturing outside my room. Scar sticks with me, and it's sweet how much he cares. "Where's Ace?" I ask.

"He went for a walk with Dodge and Mystique."

"Right." I sigh. "Has that been happening a lot since I've been locked away?"

"They get on. She feels close to him after what you all went through." The bitch in me wants to roll my eyes, but instead, I nod and smile. She wants to win him over, and right now, I feel like that's a possibility. Spotting Lucy, I make a beeline for her.

"Morning. It's great to see you up and about." She smiles, hugging me.

ACE

"It feels good," I admit. I take Abel from her, and he nuzzles into my chest. "I need to vent." I sigh, taking a seat on the couch.

"Okay, go ahead."

"Is it weird if I talk to you about Ace, because it feels weird?"

"It's not for me, unless you talk about," she pauses and glances around and then lowers her voice, "sex."

"Ugh, I don't want to talk about that," I say, covering Abel's ears. "Last night, he admitted that he loved me."

Lucy's eyes widen and she smiles. "Wow, that's huge."

"I know. The thing is, he was drunk. Like really drunk."

"Oh." It wasn't the reaction I needed, and my heart sinks further. Lucy picks up on it and rushes to reassure me. "I'm sure he meant it. People do talk the truth when drunk."

"But that's no good if he doesn't remember it today. He's acting like nothing happened."

"Have you asked him?"

"No," I almost screech. "I can't just ask him, it's embarrassing."

NICOLA JANE

"You have a right to know where you stand. These men think they can do whatever they like, and I'm sick of it. Take control and—" She's cut off when Tag storms into the clubhouse looking pissed as hell.

"Lucy Corallo," he bellows, and she groans. "You were supposed to drop my son off to me today, or did you forget again?"

"No, I didn't forget. I was bringing him later." Her voice is strong and fierce, and I'm shocked she isn't quaking in her boots as the anger rolls off Tag.

"We agreed on ten o'clock."

"You agreed, I didn't. You sent your damn monkey to arrange it while you were on a date!"

Tag half smiles. "And your point?"

"My point," she hisses, standing, "is that if you want to order me to bring your child to see you, then the least you can do is deliver the message yourself." She's so far in his face, I find myself wincing. Damn, when did this girl get so ballsy?

"You're playing a fucking game that you won't win, Lucy."

ACE

"I already am, Tag, because your son isn't where you ordered him to be, and I know that's fucking with your head." She almost looks smug, and I swear, steam comes out of his ears.

I stand, drawing both of their attention to me and Abel. "So, you went on a date?" I ask, and Tag gives me his cocky smile. "What the hell happened to you two? You love each other."

"She kicked me out."

"You deserved it," snaps Lucy.

"Ace and I don't want this. We don't want you guys fighting over what happened. Life is too short."

Lucy shuffles her feet. "He wasted no time in dating again."

"I didn't go on a date. Anton was just saying that to piss you off," mumbles Tag, and they both remind me of teenagers.

"Take a few hours to sort your shit out. I'll watch Abel. I promise not to leave the club with him."

Lucy sighs. "No, you should be resting."

"Go," I order. "I insist."

Tag takes Lucy by the hand. "Why don't we stay here? We'll go upstairs and talk. If Mae gets tired, she can bring Abel up to us." Lucy reluctantly agrees, and he drags her away.

Chapter Nineteen

♥

ACE

Doc called to update me about Mae, so I'm surprised when I get back from an hour-long walk to find her sitting with Abel and reading him a story. She looks up at me and smiles before going back to the story. I want so bad to let the world know how I feel about her, but I'm not rushing this. It needs to be perfect.

"Pres," pants Hulk, running into the clubhouse. "We need to call church, now."

It's urgent, I see it in his face, so we send a message out to all the guys, and within the hour, everyone is gathered around the large table in church. "Anton has him," blurts out Hulk. "He has Lorenzo. Tag doesn't know yet."

NICOLA JANE

I stand. "Got him where?"

"Not sure. He didn't give much away."

"So, what does he want us to do?"

"He's waiting on your instruction. He said the Mafia want him gone, doesn't care how."

"He's letting us make the kill?"

"Anton said you should get it, after what he did to you and Mae."

"Okay, I need to think about it. I want him to suffer, but I want to talk to Mae and Mystique about it."

"The other thing is, Anton seems to think the spy is one of the club girls. Something Tag's dad said."

"I need more than that, Hulk. I can't go slitting throats if I don't know who the fuck it is."

"It's something we'll need to get out of Lorenzo."

I decide to tell Mystique first. Mae is still with Abel, and she looks settled, so I don't want to ruin her smile just yet. I get Mystique in my office and she sits opposite me. "We have Lorenzo."

She inhales sharply. "I didn't think we'd ever see him again."

ACE

"You don't have to. I just thought you should know."

"What's gonna happen to him?"

"He'll die. Slow and painful, I'll make sure of it."

She nods, letting that sink in before shrugging her shoulders. "Good, I'm glad. I don't want him to hurt anyone else like that."

"I'll let you know when he's not breathing our air anymore."

"Can I be there?" I hesitate. I wasn't expecting that, and like Mae keeps pointing out, we don't know this chick. She'd be a witness, and Hulk would not be happy, plus we never allow women around club business, but I nod anyway. She deserves closure and, technically, she isn't a woman of The Rebellion yet.

Next, I call in Mae, and she leaves Abel with Scar. "Doc is pleased with your progress," I say.

"Is that why you called me in here all official?"

"No, I have some news. We have Lorenzo."

Her face pales. "Oh."

"Aren't you happy?" I was expecting her to at least look relieved, but she looks anxious.

"I'm happy he can't hurt anyone. It's what happens next that worries me."

"Why?"

"Because I know what you want to do with him."

"He deserves it, Mae," I growl.

"He does, but I want to be there, and I know what you're gonna say to that."

I fall silent, trying to get my words right. I know she needs the closure too, but as her man, *almost,* I should take care of this so she doesn't have to deal with having that on her conscience. "You know my rules on that, Mae. No women allowed around club business, especially business like that."

"How is that fair when I was the one they attacked? I should get to watch him suffer."

"You don't want those images in your head, baby. It's bad enough you stuck a screwdriver in the guy back at the house. And I know that gives you nightmares. I hear you scream out and see you wake up looking at your hands for blood."

"I need it, Ace. You know I do. Please give me this."

ACE

I hate that she looks so desperate, and any other time, I'd give her what she wants, but not this. It's for her own good. "I'm sorry, Mae, but I can't—" I'm cut off when my office door swings open and Hulk stands there looking pissed. Mystique is behind him, an expression of panic on her face.

"So, now we're letting strangers in on club business?" he growls.

I glare angrily. The last thing I need is him blurting this out before I've had a chance to explain to Mae. "Not now, Hulk, and knock before you barge right on in here with your attitude."

"As your VP, I strongly advise that we keep it club members only. It's not a spectator sport."

I groan when I see the realisation on Mae's face. "You're letting her go but not me?"

I sigh and rub at my forehead. I'm sure I feel more lines creasing there than I've ever had before. "Mae, baby—" I begin, but she puts her hand up to me.

"Nuh-uh, Ace. Whatever you say next is going to piss me off further, so just stay quiet." She folds her arms and pastes a stubborn expression on her beautiful face.

"Right, Hulk, get the fuck out." I wait for him to leave and slam the door closed. Turning to see Mae's sad expression, I almost crumble. I know how badly she wants this. "Baby, trust I know what's best for you. Right now, while you're still recovering, the last thing you need is the trauma of a murder. It isn't going to be pretty, and I don't want you to see any more than you already have."

"But it's okay for Mystique to see that? She's a stranger to this club, an outsider. What if she tells someone what you did? You'll go to jail."

"I owe her. She saved us, Mae. After this, I'm even with her, I don't owe her."

"Right. Well, you go off and play Bonnie and Clyde with a girl we hardly know, and I'll play the part of a delicate little flower who can't handle her shit."

Mae stands to leave, but I rush in front of her, blocking the door so she can't leave. "Don't go like this. I can't stand it when you're mad at me. I want to protect you. What's wrong with that?"

"I can't do this with you right now, Ace."

"You're being ridiculous. I'm the boss around here and I'm laying down the law. You know how this works."

"I thought I knew, but then I found out it only applies when it suits."

I groan. "I can't risk you being there and it all going to shit." I sigh heavily before adding, "You should also know we think one of the club girls was feeding back to him."

"Does that surprise you, Ace, when you take in anyone with a sob story? It was probably Angel. I'm sure you shared lots of secrets when you were fucking her," she spits.

"Angel wouldn't do that to me."

Mae gives an empty laugh and rubs her face, she's exhausted. "But she didn't do it to you, did she? You might have been there, but you weren't pinned down and raped. She wanted to hurt you without actually hurting you."

"It wasn't Angel," I growl, refusing to believe she'd do that.

NICOLA JANE

"I'm going for a walk. I need to clear my head. I think it's best if you sleep in your own room tonight."

I get that tight feeling in my chest. I hate the thought of not being with her at night. She still wakes continuously screaming and crying. "Take someone with you."

"I'm fine. You have the bad guy, remember."

"Damn it, Mae, stop being so fucking stubborn. I can't deal with you when you're like this."

"When I don't conform. When I don't swoon because you want to murder a man for me. Apologies if I've offended you," she spits angrily.

I drive my fist into the drywall, taking us both by surprise. It crumbles and pieces fall to the floor. "Just take someone with you," I hiss, keeping my back to her. She leaves without saying a word, but I feel the disappointment lingering in the air well after she's left the room.

MAE

I don't walk far. I get to the gate and feel my heart palpitating in my chest. Doc said I might experience panic attacks and anxiety. He talked about getting me some

ACE

counselling, but the thought of talking to a stranger about what happened scares me.

Instead of leaving the clubhouse grounds, I walk around within, since at least I feel safe here. Dodge trails behind. "You're a traitor," I say, and he wags his tail. "Walking with Mystique like that." I crouch down and ruffle his ears while he tries to lick my face.

I stand when Lucy approaches. It's nice to finally see a smile on her face. "Thanks for that, Mae."

"All sorted then?"

"We talked." She gives me a sheepish grin, and I guess that means they did a little more than talk. "Ace is speaking with Tag. It looked important."

"I may as well tell you, they found Tag's dad."

"Oh, well, that's good news, isn't it?"

"I guess."

"You don't look so sure."

"I dunno. I should feel happy, but I don't. Anton wants him dead and has given the rights to Ace. I want to be there, but Ace said no."

Lucy chews on her lower lip. "Does it matter who's there and who pulls the trigger as long as he's dead?"

"Since when did you come over to the dark side?" Lucy isn't one for violence. She still cringes throughout Tag's fights.

She laughs. "Tag must be rubbing off on me."

"Growing up in the MC makes you immune to sex and violence. My mum always tried to shield me from that stuff, but you hear the guys talking and it becomes normal. I've never had a murder on my hands up until recently. But I don't feel bad for killing that guy, Luce. He deserved it, and so does Lorenzo, but I should get the rights for his murder. I know that'll never be allowed, so the least Ace should allow me is to be there when it happens."

"Why doesn't he want you there?"

"He said he doesn't think I can handle it while I'm recovering still. I think it'll help. Besides, Mystique's allowed to be there."

Lucy raises her eyebrows. "Ouch, bet that hurt." I shrug. Of course, it did, but saying it out loud sounds pathetic.

ACE

The rumble of motorcycle engines interrupts our conversation, then the gate slides open and Scar steps out from the gate hut. "That looks like a lot of the guys. Something going down?" I ask.

"I dunno. Tag didn't say anything."

We wait for them to park up and then head inside. There must be thirty more guys who turned up, and with the ones already inside, it's busy. Tag heads over. "Get dolled up, girls. Party tonight."

"Party for what?" I ask.

"Pres never said, just that all the guys were coming together."

Piper rushes over, looking excited. "Great news. It's been too long since we all got together like this."

"What's so big that it calls for everyone to be here?" I ask.

"Who cares? We need to get dressed up, girls. I'll grab us some wine, you girls head up to my room."

Those damn heart palpitations come back. The thought of being with everyone is nice, but it makes me nervous. *Do they all know what happened to me? Will they be talking about it?* I shake the anxiety away. It's messing with my head. These guys know me, and they love me like their sister.

An hour later, I sip on my glass of wine while Piper holds up various outfits from her large collection of clothes. "The good thing about seeing a Mafia boss is that he throws money at me constantly." She holds up a Vera Wang dress, and we all touch it like it's gold.

"It's so pretty." Lucy sighs. It's not like she isn't used to designer things. Coming from a wealthy background herself, and being married to Tag, she's not short of money or pretty things.

"How's Hulk taking it?" I ask, and Piper shoves the dress back into her wardrobe.

"Not great. He's just mad that I'm not waiting around for his calls no more."

"I get the impression he really likes you," says Lucy.

"Hulk only likes himself, everyone else he uses for fun to entertain himself. If I was still showing an interest in him, he'd be treating me like he used to, pure shit. He just doesn't like to lose, especially to Anton. And I gave him the chance to tell me how he felt. I said if he didn't tell me, then I'd move on."

"He's not the kind of man to be backed into a corner," I point out.

"Well, I'm not a call girl. I deserve better, and he told me he couldn't commit, and so here we are. Anton's a nice guy. He doesn't show it, but when we're together, he's so sweet."

Lucy rolls her eyes. "Ugh, Anton and sweet in the same sentence." She shudders, and we laugh.

"And he'll protect me, no matter what. Even when he's mad at me, he's checking in with me. He cares, yah know."

I smile. "If you're happy, that's all that matters, Pip."

She throws a dress my way, and I catch it and hold it out. It's short, almost like a shirt style with buttons down the front. It reminds me of the white shirt I wore, and I place it on the bed and sigh. "I don't know if I'm okay to go to this party tonight, girls."

They both look at me confused. "You have to come, Mae. It won't be the same without you."

"It just doesn't feel right."

NICOLA JANE

Piper takes my hand and pulls me to stand. "Mae, we aren't saying you have to get over this. We haven't brushed it under the carpet. If you need to talk to us about what happened, we're here. But don't lock yourself away. You don't need to hide from everyone. We all love you so much, and what happened, it breaks our hearts. You need to surround yourself with everyone who loves you, and tonight, everyone in that room loves you."

A tear slips down my face and I smile. "Thanks Pip."

"So, get yourself made up, dress in pyjamas for all we care, but you have to be there." I nod. I'll try, for them.

Chapter Twenty

ACE

I stretch out, pulling my neck from side to side and then cracking my knuckles. I'm full of tension but so ready for this. Anton slides back the garage door, and we all follow him inside. He pulls back a trap door, and we exchange a look that says we're all feeling a little on edge at stepping into the Mafia boss's dungeon. I'd heard the rumour that Anton's dad, Conner, had this dug out especially for things like this. No one can hear you scream deep underground.

The steps seem to go on forever, deeper and deeper, until we finally hit the bottom. It smells of damp and earth, and it's cold. The tunnel leads us to a door that's bolted shut.

NICOLA JANE

Anton's right-hand man, Michael, puts in the code and it pops open.

Inside, the room is dark and silent. I'm wondering if Lorenzo is already dead just because it's so cold down here. Mystique slips her hand into mine and leans into me. I give it a reassuring squeeze.

Anton flicks a switch and a dim light flickers. In the corner of the room, tied to a wooden stool, is Lorenzo. He doesn't look so smug right now, and I smile in satisfaction. Mystique curls into me, and I wrap an arm around her shoulder. She's shivering, though I'm not sure if that's from the cold or the fact she's scared just from seeing this piece of shit.

"You had to bring your pussies to back you up," says Lorenzo, smirking.

"No, I was happy to get one of my men to slit your throat. But then you went and made it all personnel, and now there's a line of people who want in on your murder," drawls Anton, his tone flat and bored. "I should have sold tickets."

ACE

"Can we hurry this up? We have a party to get to." We all turn at the sound of Tag's voice. We didn't expect him to come. I'd told him earlier that Anton had Lorenzo, but he hadn't said much. After all, he's still his father. "Hey, Pops, you don't look so good."

"Matteo," says Lorenzo, almost in a whisper.

"You didn't think I'd come to see this?" Tag asks Anton, shaking his hand.

"He's your father," sighs Anton, "I didn't want to put you in that position."

Tag steps closer to Lorenzo. There's something different about the look in his eyes, and I can see why people fear Matteo Corallo, in and out of the cage.

"He tried to have me killed and then he planned to take my wife," he spits, then turns to Lorenzo. "I've waited a long time to see you suffer."

"It's our way of life, Matteo. It wasn't personal."

"Are you serious? I'm your fucking son! It doesn't get more personal than that. I tried to help you. I lied to Conner to keep your waste of space arse alive!"

NICOLA JANE

"Do it, kill me. You'll spend the rest of your days and nights remembering this moment," growls Lorenzo, pulling hard on the ropes holding him to the chair. Tag punches him, it's fast and unexpected, but Lorenzo's smirks, his lip bleeding. "You still hit like an untrained, feral pussy."

"Full of encouragement. You were always so positive."

"You were nothing before I put you in that cage," Lorenzo yells.

"I was a fucking kid. You didn't want a son, you wanted a killing machine."

"And you failed at that. You're gonna let that biker piece of shit slit my throat? The mafia affiliated with biker scum . . ." He spits on the ground angrily. "Conner would turn in his grave."

"Conner was a piece of shit, just like you. We've never been so well off. The power we have is more than you could ever have dreamed of."

"Ella was always a whore. Even as a child, she'd use those big eyes to get what she wanted. Can you blame a man going there?" He's referring to Anton's sister, who suffered sexual abuse at the hands of her father for years and they never knew. When she finally told everyone, Anton shot him dead.

Anton steps forward, a growl leaving his throat. Tag stops him. "Don't. He wants you to kill him quick. Stick to the plan."

That's my cue to step forward, Mystique by my side. "I told you I'd kill you," I say. "The most satisfying thing," I continue, pulling out my blade slowly as I speak, "is that now I know just how you feel about bikers, it makes it all the more sweet."

"Fuck you. Your bitch was worth it. That tight pussy begged to feel a real man."

I breathe deep, calming myself. I will kill him slow and painfully, just like I promised, but he's trying to provoke me so that I make it quick.

I stab the blade into his hand. He can't move it away because it's bound by ropes to the arm of the chair. He grits his teeth but doesn't make a sound. "I love the feel of flesh breaking." I sigh, satisfaction ripping through me.

"We should leave you to it," says Anton. "The smell is making me want to join in."

Footsteps retreat from the room. "Can I stay?" It's Mystique. I nod once, beginning to get lost in a frenzy of cutting.

I slump against the wall exhausted. I'm not sure how long we've been down here but it feels like hours. There's blood coating my hands and arms. I'm short of breath, and my mind is lost in visions of Mae and the men who hurt her. I feel a light touch on my forearm, and I flinch before realising it's Mystique. She takes the bloodied knife from my hand and steps towards Lorenzo. He passed out some time ago, the pain becoming too much for him, and now, the blood loss will keep him weak and subdued until he finally bleeds to death.

I lean my head back against the damp wall and watch as Mystique lifts the knife and brings it down hard, plunging it into his chest. Lorenzo sucks in a breath and releases slowly, the air rattling around his chest and then it goes

ACE

silent. The knife clatters to the floor, and Mystique brings her hands to her mouth in shock. I push myself to stand, and she falls back into my arms, sobbing hard. "Shh, it's okay," I whisper, placing a gentle kiss on her head.

"I didn't mean to." She pauses, crying harder. "I just wanted to..."

"It's okay. He can't ever hurt anyone ever again."

She turns in my arms and buries her face in my chest. I hold her, watching the lifeless body of Lorenzo Corallo. He deserved the slow, painful death that I gave him. I don't feel any type of guilt for him, and I know that when I leave this room, I won't ever think of this moment again.

MAE

I stir my drink with a straw. The party has been in full swing for the last three hours, but Ace, Tag, Hulk, Scar, Anton, and Mystique are nowhere to be seen. "You look lovely, Mae," says Piper for the hundredth time, she's acting odd.

"Where are they all?" I ask. "Do you think it has anything to do with Tag's dad?"

Piper shrugs. "Who cares about that arsehole, Mae?"

Tag steps into the clubhouse and heads straight for the bar. He orders a double whiskey straight and my heart sinks. "Where's Ace?" I ask.

"He went round back," he mutters, knocking the amber liquid back and wincing.

The only reason the men use the back door is because they don't want to be seen by passing eyes. "He'll be here, Mae. Let him sort himself out," suggests Piper.

I push off the bar and head for Ace's room. I need to know either way if Lorenzo is dead. Taking the stairs two at a time, Piper follows me, trying to talk me into going back downstairs to the party.

I get to his door, but Piper steps in front of me. "Before you go in there, just remember he loves you. Whatever state he's in, he needs your support right now." I've seen Ace after a murder many times before. He goes into a dark mood and he's hard to reach for a few hours. I'll know if he killed Lorenzo. I push past her and shove the door open. Ace is sitting on the edge of his bed, his head hung low and his elbows rested on his knees. He looks up, and we lock eyes. He's covered in blood. It stains his arms, his hands, his clothes, and there's splatters on his face.

"Do you have any shampoo that doesn't smell like men?" comes Mystique's voice from the bathroom.

My eyes widen, and Ace stands looking panicked. "Mae, it isn't how it looks."

I nod, but my face can't hide how I feel, and he sees the hurt in my eyes. "Is he dead?" Ace hesitates and then nods once. "And she helped you?" He nods again.

"It's good news that he's dead, isn't it, Mae?" asks Piper brightly.

"Bonded by blood," I mutter. Ace once told me that he killed a man who tried to attack Hulk's mum. It was a long time ago, and she was in a back alley with some drunk guy who wouldn't take no for an answer. Ace had been in the right place at the right time and killed the guy. He said from that night on, he and Hulk's mum had never separated. They'd been bonded by blood.

"Fuck you, Mae," he growls. "It wasn't like that. I wanted to protect you."

NICOLA JANE

We all turn to stare as Mystique comes into the room, dripping from her shower and naked, not even a towel covering her beautiful body. My eyes almost pop out of my head, and she smiles guiltily at me. "Sorry, I didn't hear you guys come in."

"Clearly," mutters Piper.

"It's fine. We'll leave you to it." I turn on my heel and stomp towards my room. I didn't want to party in the first place, and now, I feel even less in the mood.

"I honestly don't think anything is going on between the two of them, Mae," Piper says. "He looked just as shocked as we did."

"You know what, I don't even care that she's in his room naked. She's trouble, and she's trying to wriggle her way in there with him. By letting her shower in his room and always having her hang around, he's asking for it. He takes her on something so secret but leaves me here, what message is that giving her?"

There's a banging on my door and I know instantly it's Ace. "Mae, open the fucking door."

ACE

I pull it open, and Ace is breathing heavy, a sign that he's pissed. "I'm gonna shower and then we're gonna go downstairs and party."

"I am not partying with you. Take *Mystie*. You seem to want to take her everywhere else."

He pushes past me and drops a fresh set of clothes on the bed. "I want to take you."

He disappears into my bathroom, and I hear the shower turn on.

"As tempting as it is to peek a look at our naked President, I'm gonna leave you two to fight it out. Try not to mess up your makeup." Piper kisses me on the cheek and leaves.

I watch sulkily from my spot on the bed as Ace dresses, all traces of blood gone. He smells good, and I have an internal pep talk to remind myself that just minutes ago, he was covered in another man's blood.

He holds out his hand. "Let's go."

"I'm not in the mood to party, Ace. Can you even understand why I'm so mad with you?"

"Walk or I will throw you over my shoulder." He isn't kidding around—he has a dark look in his eye.

"I get you wanted to protect me, that you felt this overriding need to control the situation, but to take her and not me, that was a shit move, Ace."

He sighs, suddenly looking tired. "I need to protect you. I couldn't back then, but I can now. I told you I'd be overbearing and I'd drive you crazy, but you said you didn't care. You said I should try. So, here I am, Mae, I'm trying. I'll get it wrong, but I don't think I did this time. I don't care that Mystique might lay awake remembering every splatter of blood for the next month, but I care that you might. Lorenzo is dead, it doesn't matter how, and it doesn't matter who was there. I took care of that for you, so you didn't have those images. I wasn't trying to push you out or put her first."

I hang my head. I know it wasn't his intention, but it still hurts. "I'm still mad. You need to distance yourself from her. You might not see it, but she's trying to worm her way into your heart."

ACE

He gives a lopsided smile and holds out his hand, "Are you gonna walk or should I carry you?"

Once downstairs, he shakes hands and greets various other bikers. Some of them we don't often see because they're based elsewhere. I go to move away from him, but he snakes his arm around my shoulders and pulls me back to him. "People will start to ask questions, Ace," I hiss. It's a moment I've waited for, but it feels weird, especially as we've still not discussed last night.

"Good." Ace pushes a drink into my hand and then continues to talk to Trucker. I spot Mystique across the room chatting with Queenie. She watches us, occasionally looking back to Queenie, but always returning her stare to us. Ace finally finishes his conversation with Trucker and then pulls me towards the bar. "Stay there, don't move," he orders and then pulls himself to stand on the bar top. He whistles to get everyone's attention.

"Thanks for coming," he begins as the chatter dies down. "You're probably all wondering why I called you here. After the last few weeks, things have been tense, and I thought we could all do with some good news." He jumps down from the bar and stands next to me. "I'm not getting any younger, so I thought it was about time I took claim to a fantastic, amazing woman." I stare at him in disbelief, shocked that he'd do this without speaking to me. There're a few cheers among The Rebellion. "Mae wasn't on my radar. We've always been friends, and she's the one I'd go to if I couldn't handle shit, so I don't know why it took me so long to see it. She's everything our kind of men need in an old lady. So," he smiles down at me, "meet my old lady."

He takes my hand and holds it up for everyone to see. The room erupts with joy, and we're enveloped in hugs as I'm pulled from Ace and spun around by various men. My heart hammers in my chest as I'm congratulated. My mum wraps me in her arms. "Are you okay with this?" I ask.

"I'm happy if you are." She smiles, kissing my cheek. "He's a good man, Mae, and he'll take care of you."

"I wasn't expecting him to do that," I mutter. "We still have so much to sort out."

ACE

She hugs me again. "After all the bad stuff you've been through, it's nice to have something positive. Enjoy it, Mae. Stop looking for the bad in it. You can sort everything out as you go along."

Ace joins us, kissing me on the cheek and wrapping his arm around me. "You thought I'd forgotten about last night and what I said to you?"

I nod. "Maybe."

"You can stop worrying about other women. I'm all yours, baby." He places another kiss, this time on my lips. "I love you."

Butterflies dart around inside my stomach as I smile. "I love you too." And I do.

But Lorenzo isn't forgotten about. I can't let it go as easily as he can.

Chapter Twenty-One

ACE

I take the drink that Hulk hands me and then, when he isn't watching, I put it on a nearby table. Drinking after a kill like that, brings me down and I'll get lost in dark thoughts. I want happy memories of me and Mae this evening. I glance over to where my old lady sits on the couch. She's tired and looks pale. A party was pushing her when she was still recovering.

I head over and crouch down in front of her. "You ready for bed?" Nodding, she takes my hand, and we sneak off.

ACE

The party will continue until the early hours of the morning, and no one will miss us now the alcohol is flowing.

We go to Mae's room and undress in silence. Mae goes to the bathroom, and I slip into bed. I don't want to push her too much, and I don't want her to think I expect anything from her. She isn't ready. I turn away from her side of the bed and pull the covers right up. When she finally gets into bed, she turns the light out and snuggles down too. There's a large space between us. It isn't how I imagined our first night together as an official couple.

We're asleep for less than an hour before her crying wakes me. She's shaking and whimpering as I sit up and turn the lamp on. "Mae," I whisper. "Mae, wake up." She begins to thrash about, crying out louder, so I gently place my hand on her arm. "Mae, you're safe, I'm here."

She stills and snuggles down into her pillow. The rest of the night is pretty much the same, and by the time the sun rises, I'm exhausted. I wait until she steps into the shower and then decide to go for a run. Last night's activities play on my mind, but I need to fight the darkness that threatens to overtake me.

NICOLA JANE

Dodge runs beside me for a solid half-hour before he sits down and refuses to run anymore. I threaten to put him on a diet, and we walk back to the clubhouse.

The place is a mess, bodies sleeping on the couches and the floor. Empty glasses and bottles are strewn across every surface. I slam the door as I enter, and a few of the guys sit up and look around confused. "Get this shithole cleaned up," I yell as I march for my office.

A minute later, Hulk comes in. "You okay, Pres?"

"Fucking great."

"You wanna talk?"

I shake my head and sink back into my chair. "Women are confusing. One minute, you think you have them all figured out, but turns out, you really don't."

Hulk sits on my couch. "If you still haven't worked them out, then what chance have I got?" He laughs to himself and pops a cigarette into his mouth before chucking the pack to me.

"Mae's acting weird."

"She was pissed at you for everything that went down with Lorenzo. You knew that before you claimed her."

"How long does a woman usually stay pissed for?"

"In your case, probably a while. Go and talk to her, Pops. Mae's someone you can talk to."

"And say what? I thought she'd be happy he was dead. I explained why I didn't want her there. I admit I fucked up by letting Mystique be there, but I can't change that now. I close my eyes and see what they did to her, and it makes me so mad that I want to smash shit up. It's not her fault, she didn't choose it, but I still can't help feeling lost and jealous and hurt."

"It's natural. No one wants to see that shit."

"But I feel jealous. How is that okay?"

"It was still another man with the woman you love. You can't help how your mind reacts to it."

"Mae thinks Angel is the spy."

"I can't lie, it crossed my mind too."

"Really?" I trust Hulk, he's good at reading people, but I find it so hard to believe that Angel would do that to me.

"She has the motive. If she wanted to fuck up you and Mae, and then Lorenzo came at her with a plan where they could both walk away happy, I think she'd go for that."

I shake my head. "I don't buy it. She wasn't that into me, not enough to screw me over knowing what would happen if I found out."

"Then ask her straight. After last night's public claiming, I'm sure she'll gladly try to hurt you with the truth."

Hulk goes to the door and shouts for Angel. She appears, all smiles. "Everything okay?" she asks.

Hulk glares at me. "Pres needs to talk with you. Take a seat." She sits, and he stands by my side. "Lorenzo is dead," he says coldly.

"What?" She almost gasps, and I groan. "I mean, who's Lorenzo?"

"Too late," growls Hulk. "You'd better get talking."

Angel bursts into tears. "I'm sorry," she cries. "It wasn't supposed to get that far."

I stand, my chair falling back and hitting the wall. I didn't expect her to crack so easily. "I stood up for you. I told Hulk and Mae that it wasn't you, that you wouldn't do that to me."

"I didn't mean to. He tricked me."

ACE

"Even if that was true, you should have come to me." I head for the door. "Do what you think needs doing, Hulk. I need to be with my woman."

Angel is no threat to me now, not with Lorenzo dead, and if it happened like she said, he was using her for intel. Hulk will kick her ass out. No more free riding from the club.

MAE

The bedroom door slams back against the wall, and I glance over my shoulder to see Ace standing in the doorway looking pissed. I was upset when I saw he'd gone this morning, I wanted to talk with him about the whole Lorenzo thing, and I needed to talk about why we both went to sleep last night with our backs to each other. "You look tired," I say, rolling onto my side to face him.

"How do I stop the nightmares, Mae? What can I do to make them leave your head?"

"Talk to me," I say simply.

"Where do I start?" he asks, stepping into the room and closing the door. Dodge jumps onto the end of the bed and curls up. "I want to talk about it, but I don't want to make you relive it. I don't want to talk to Hulk because it's not my place to tell people what happened to you." He sits on the bed and takes my hand in his. "We should be happy, but I feel like this big shadow is hanging over us, Mae."

"Me too," I admit. "I feel ashamed. I don't dare touch you in case all you see is me having sex with that man."

"Jesus," he hisses, wincing at my words. "You didn't have sex with him. You were raped. It's completely different."

"Was it different in your eyes?"

"How can you even ask that? I'm scared to touch you in case I trigger you, but don't think for one minute that I don't want to. It's all I can think about. Do you know how hard it's been lying next to you each night and not being able to touch you the way I want to?"

"I want you to touch me. Ace, I need your touch to wipe away theirs."

"I don't want to push you too far. When you're ready, you have to make the move, baby."

ACE

I nod, acknowledging that I'll do that when I feel ready. "I'm glad Lorenzo is dead. I wanted to say thank you, but it seemed weird." I smile. "But thanks."

"I'm sorry for taking Mystique. I get why you were pissed about it. I'll try to listen more when you're trying to make me see where I've fucked up. And you were right about Angel. She was feeding information back to Lorenzo."

"Shit," I mutter. I thought she had the motive, but actually finding out I was right is still a shock. "Sorry, Ace, I know you've spent a lot of time with her. The betrayal must hurt."

"I should know by now that the two people closest to me are usually always right," he adds a smile.

"Hulk called it too?"

Ace nods. "Yeah. I told him what you said, and he agreed."

"Wow, Hulk and I agreeing on something." I smile, and Ace laughs.

"Is it too soon to get him to call you stepmum?" jokes Ace, and I shudder at the thought. We're similar in age, and I don't think either of us are ready for that title. "We need to make you my old lady."

"I thought we did that already?"

"I need your name on my skin, baby, and if you're comfortable with it, I'd like you to have my name too." It's sweet that he asks me instead of telling me. I know it's usually customary to be 'tagged' as belonging to a biker, and I'd love nothing more than to have Ace on my skin. It means he's serious, and knowing that makes me happier than I've felt in a long time.

I lean towards him and wrap my arms around his neck. I place a kiss on his lips and smile. "I'd love to."

He grins. "Great, I'll go call my guy. Get dressed. Doc is coming any minute to give you another check-up."

I wait for Doc to arrive. He does his usual tests, blood pressure, weight, etcetera. I insist on another pregnancy test, which he does. "I really don't think you have to worry, Mae. Everything has come back clear, along with this pregnancy test. You can relax."

I nod. "Actually, Doc, while I have you here, I was thinking about what you said about talking to someone, a counsellor. I'm still having nightmares throughout the night."

He packs away his equipment. "I can arrange that for you. It's a good idea."

"This is an odd question, knowing what I've been through. But am I good to go, in the bedroom area, I mean?" I feel my cheeks redden and look down. "Or should I wait for a set amount of time to make sure I'm healed?"

"Mae, it isn't an odd question. Everyone handles this stuff differently. Just because you're not rocking in the shower sobbing doesn't mean you're odd. You're ready to go when you feel ready. It may be wise to take it slow. The first time might bring back memories and it may freak you out, but it's all normal."

"I feel like I need to move forward," I admit, feeling relieved he didn't judge me.

"As long as it's at your own pace, you'll be fine."

I know Ace won't ever push me into sex. He won't lay a finger on me until he's certain I'm ready. Part of me needs to see if I can do it without freaking, and now we're official, it seems the next progressive step towards our future together.

Chapter Twenty-Two

ACE

Life has a funny way of completely changing direction. I was settled, not worrying about taking an old lady or playing house, yet here I am with someone I've known for a long time, claiming her.

The needle brushes over my skin, but I relish the sting as it pushes ink there, marking Mae's name into my arm forever. It was unexpected, but it feels right. Nothing has ever felt so certain, and as I watch her look down at her own ink, I smile. My name on her wrist looks good, and it sends a buzz through my veins. She is mine.

"I have to say," smiles Tatts, "I never thought I'd see this day, Pres."

"She's crazy for taking me on," I agree, "but now it's written in ink, it's forever." Her eyes fix on mine, noting the change in my familiar saying. "Ink is permanent, blood can be washed away," I add.

"That's true," says Tatts, laying the ink gun down and then wiping my arm. "All done, brother." We shake hands.

I place a gentle kiss on Mae's lips before guiding her toward the exit. "Let's get home, old lady." I smile. The words roll off my tongue so naturally, I wonder if I'll ever get bored of saying them.

We get back to the clubhouse, and Mae goes to show her new ink to her mum and the girls. I take a seat at the bar, and Hulk hands me a drink. "It's good to see Mae looking so happy, Pops."

"Yeah, it is," I nod, "but you don't look so happy lately. How're things with you and Piper?"

Hulk shrugs. We don't usually do these deep conversations, but he looks so miserable since he found out she's been seeing Anton. "It's my own fault. I shouldn't have treated her the way I did."

"Have you told her that?"

He shakes his head. "She doesn't give me the time of day just lately. Always off with him."

"Then pin her down, so she has to listen."

"Not my style. Besides, Anton wouldn't be happy, and I don't want to cause tensions when things are good between us and them."

I agree, things are going well between us and the alliance is working out. Money is flowing, and we have a mutual respect for each other to the point where they can come and go from the clubhouse like they're members.

Scar passes us. We watch him leave, and then I turn to Hulk. "Did you know that he helps at a shelter?"

Hulk laughs. "Since when?"

"Not sure. Mae told me. Some place for battered women, I think."

"Well, his mum was in a violent relationship when he was a kid. Didn't she die that way?" I shrug. Scar doesn't talk much about his past. It's something I want to discuss with him, but I don't think he'd appreciate it. Most of the guys are private about that shit. "He's been gone a lot lately, so that explains it."

Piper comes through the door laden down with bags. Hulk rolls his eyes and turns his back to her. "Been shopping?" I ask.

Anton steps in behind her, also carrying bags. "This woman is a shopaholic," he groans.

"You letting the Mafia buy your shit?" snaps Hulk, letting his jealousy get the better of him.

"I can treat my woman to whatever she likes," says Anton with a smirk. "Maybe you should have done this, then she wouldn't have gotten tired of your arse."

Hulk growls. "I wasn't talking to you."

"What the hell did you just say," I mutter in Hulk's direction, "about keeping things calm between you guys."

Piper sighs. "Let's go to my room, Anton," she says, breezing past us with her head held high.

"You need to stop ignoring me, Piper," growls Hulk angrily. He waits a beat before adding, "Or I'll tell him everything." Piper stops in her tracks and spins to face him.

All eyes turn to Hulk but he's fixed on her, waiting for her to speak.

"Piper," Anton says, "what the hell's he talking about?"

Book 3

Anton

is coming soon...

A note from me to you

♥

I was dubious about re-releasing this series. When I read it back, I realised I've come a long way since these books were released. However, lots of readers still contact me about this series and ask when the next one is, so i figured I'd edit it and release it because some of my readers love it.

If you read this book and hated it, please don't give up on me. It was written very early on in my writing journey. Flick to the next page and give some of my most recent books a try. A personal favourite of mine is Maverick and Scar from The Perished Riders MC.

Books by Nicola Jane

The Rebellion Series

Tag

Ace

The Kings Reapers MC

Riggs' Ruin

Capturing Cree

Wrapped in Chains

Saving Blu

Riggs' Saviour

NICOLA JANE

Taming Blade

Misleading Lake

Surviving Storm

Ravens Place

Playing Vinn

<u>The Perished Riders MC</u>

Maverick

Scar

Grim

Ghost

Dice

Arthur

<u>The Hammers MC (Splintered Hearts Series)</u>

Cooper

Kain

Tanner

Printed in Dunstable, United Kingdom